Brave the Storm

Also From Lisa Mondello

Brave the Storm
By Lisa Mondello

Rising Storm
Season 2
Episode 3

Story created by Julie Kenner and Dee Davis

EVIL EYE
CONCEPTS

Brave the Storm, Episode 3
Rising Storm, Season 2
Copyright 2016 Julie Kenner and Dee Davis Oberwetter
ISBN: 978-1-942299-95-0

Published by Evil Eye Concepts, Incorporated

Foreword

Dear reader –

We have wanted to do a project together for over a decade, but nothing really jelled until we started to toy with a kernel of an idea that sprouted way back in 2012 … and ultimately grew into Rising Storm.

We are both excited about and proud of this project—not only of the story itself, but also the incredible authors who have helped bring the world and characters we created to life.

We hope you enjoy visiting Storm, Texas. Settle in and stay a while!

Happy reading!

Julie Kenner & Dee Davis

Sign up for the Rising Storm/1001 Dark Nights Newsletter
and be entered to win an exclusive lightning bolt necklace specially
designed for Rising Storm by Janet Cadsawan of Cadsawan.com.

Go to www.RisingStormBooks.com to subscribe.

As a bonus, all subscribers will receive a free
Rising Storm story
Storm Season: Ginny & Jacob – the Prequel
by Dee Davis

Chapter One

Coming home wasn't supposed to be so hard. Chase Johnson eased himself into a chair on the porch and gazed out at the wide spread of the ranch he'd grown up on. He picked up his guitar and held it in his hands. The instrument had always been more like an extension of his arms. A music reviewer who'd seen him play at the Ryman had once said that Chase played as if he'd been born holding that guitar in his hands. Most nights it felt that way.

But that had changed a few months ago. A visit to his doctor, a few tests, and it was like his arms had been ripped from his body.

Closing his eyes, he placed his left hand on the neck of the guitar and fingered a G chord. With his right hand, he held a pick between his thumb and two fingers and steadied the tip on the G string. He paused, listening to the slight scraping of the pick against the string as he waited for the trembling in his hand to stop.

Except it didn't. He knew it wouldn't.

With the back of his hand, Chase wiped the sweat on his upper lip as dread filled him. He'd been assured that although his Parkinson's would get worse eventually, the longer he kept his music, the longer he could hold "eventually" off.

But now …

Well, apparently "eventually" had caught up to him.

Chuckling with no humor, he placed his beloved instrument in the guitar case and locked it. Nashville had been his home for more years than Storm had been. But Storm, Texas, had always been in his heart. It would always be home. His family was here.

And Anna Mae.

Chase may not have lived on the ranch all these years but after the short time being home, he already knew he still had a whole lot of fences to mend.

* * * *

"We're sliding." Sebastian Rush sat behind his desk at his campaign headquarters in Storm, his most recent polling numbers mocking him from his desktop.

Marylee scowled at him from her perch on the chair across from him. "If I hadn't stopped smoking years ago, I'd be chain smoking now. You realize your stupidity may cost us the election."

"Mother," Sebastian warned. Her tantrums over his indiscretions with Dakota Alvarez and Ginny Moreno had become a broken record that tormented him week after week after week. "It happened. Rehashing it every time we face a dip in the polls isn't going to make it go away."

"*Everything* will go away if we don't figure out a way to salvage this campaign before you sink any lower."

Marylee pushed herself up from her chair and moved to the window. There wasn't a wrinkle on her suit. Every hair on her head was in place. Just like always.

After a moment, she turned to him and cast him the disapproving glare that had become habit. "You were the golden boy, Sebastian. Ever since you were a little boy I knew you were destined for great things and I was prepared to lead you there. And you pay me back by rolling around in the mud with the trash of Storm."

He stayed quiet, familiar enough with the tirade to know she'd wind down soon enough.

"And what if Ginny Moreno really is carrying your baby? The press will eat you alive."

"The baby won't be born until after the election. I'll already be safely in office."

"That remains to be seen," she sniffed. "And even then,

Ginny's spawn can still damage your career. We have to plan for that possibility even while we fight to win this election."

She was right, even though Sebastian didn't want to hear it. Damn, if he had only known there was a possibility the baby she was carrying was his, he could have made it go away. But it was too late for that. Now her family had rallied around her. And there was no way she'd give up the baby. She was too determined to believe it was Jacob Salt's. Not that there was a chance in hell of that being true.

"We'll figure out a way to spin it, Mother. We always do."

"Sebastian, what we need is a distraction. Oliver agrees," she added, referring to Oliver Stayton, the political consultant she'd brought in to clean up this mess. So far, Sebastian had to admit the man knew what he was doing.

"What do you have in mind?"

She sat down again and crossed her legs. "Everyone loves a hero and we have our very own right here in Storm. I think we should call on Logan Murphy again."

Sebastian sighed and tossed the pen he'd been twirling between his fingers on the blotter on the desk. "He's been lukewarm at best regarding helping my candidacy. Given his connection with Ginny Moreno, I'm not sure that's the best course of action."

"They broke up."

"Yes, but I've seen him looking at her. The kid may not know it, but he's still pining for her."

Marylee's lips curled into a smile. "Doesn't matter. That's what news editing is for. He's exactly the type of positive press we need. We just have to get the footage and then we can turn it into the perfect sound bite. We get Logan on the air to show your support for veterans, and that's what people will be talking about. Not the fact that you can't keep your damn pants zipped."

Sebastian scowled, but he had to hand it to his mother. She was a master at turn-around play. And her plan could work if they could get Logan Murphy to cooperate.

"I'll have my assistant give Logan a call."

"No. You handle it personally. And soon. We need to stop this before it has a chance to get any worse."

Chapter Two

Anna Mae sat at the kitchen table with a pad of paper and a sharpened pencil. Her coffee cup had long been drained, but her mind was still cluttered with things she didn't want to think about.

Chase Johnson.

"Are you going to hang around this house brooding all day again?" Rita Mae asked, dropping the last of the morning dishes into the dishwasher.

Most of the guests they'd had overnight had either checked out or gone about their business of the day. The house was quiet and Anna Mae was ready to dive into a long list of tasks she'd written out on a notepad last night before bed.

"What are you talking about?" Anna Mae asked as she reviewed her list. She knew. She always knew. Anna Mae just wasn't in the mood for another one of Rita Mae's lectures.

Mary Louise came into the kitchen dressed more formally for the day than she normally did. "I'm not sure when I'll be home tonight," she said.

Rita Mae tilted a curious eyebrow. "Oh, no? Why not?"

"Why is she not sure or why won't she be home?" Anna Mae asked.

"Both."

"Leave the girl alone. She's young. She's probably got herself a hot date." Anna Mae winked at her niece.

Mary Louise grabbed a glass from the cabinet and then went to the refrigerator and poured some orange juice before answering. "I could say the same of you."

"Me?" Anna Mae laughed. "Don't be ridiculous. I'm too old for *hot* dates."

"Don't say that. Please don't say that," Mary Louise said. "I can't bear the thought that romance dies and love goes stale as we get older. I haven't even had a real turn at it."

"Oh, so it *is* a hot date," Rita Mae said. "I saw you talking with Tate Johnson at the barbeque yesterday. Are you seeing him?"

"It's a meeting. That's all. Tate and Hannah broke up and we're…we're just friends."

"But you'd like it to be more?" Rita Mae asked.

Mary Louise shrugged as a blush crept up her cheeks. "Besides, now that Chase Johnson is back in town, why shouldn't you have a hot date, Anna Mae?"

Anna Mae dropped the pencil she'd been holding. "Why would you say something like that?" she said, feigning ignorance.

"Oh, come on. It may have been a long time ago but Daddy told me you and Chase were once an item. I even saw an old picture of the two of you hugging."

"You did?" Rita Mae asked.

"Yeah. Daddy and Chase were both playing at some club. It didn't look like much more than a rinky-dink honkytonk. That's what my mother used to call them. Of course, Mom had a thing for hanging out with Daddy at those honkytonks. Do you remember, Anna Mae?"

There were too many places like that to remember which one Mary Louise could be talking about. Too many late nights with too much drink and too many years that made it all fuzzy now.

And she could lie to herself about how much she remembered, but Anna Mae had made a career of silently cataloguing all those moments with Chase Johnson. Perhaps that's why her anger had grown exponentially over the years after she'd told him to leave. She could have stopped him. And he would have stayed. She was sure of that. They'd loved each other so very much.

But Anna Mae couldn't bear the thought that eventually his love for her would have turned to resentment. Playing music had always been his dream. And if she'd trapped him in Storm, he'd never have truly been happy. Her brother had tried that and it had ended in divorce, and Mary Louise being more Anna and Rita Mae's daughter than his.

Would it have been different if Anna Mae had followed Chase to Nashville? It was a question that she'd rolled over in her mind for many years on many nights while missing the feel of Chase's arms around her.

"Anna Mae?"

She turned her attention to her sister, who was staring at her from across the kitchen. Her mind had wandered to a time when she was younger than Mary Louise. Despite the fact that she hadn't had her happily-ever-after with Chase, that didn't mean that Mary Louise couldn't have that.

"To be honest, when I was a girl, I went to so many music halls I can't even count them. Your father was quite the musician." She stifled a sigh of regret because she didn't want to feel it. She wanted to remember times that were happy and those late nights with her brother and Chase playing *were* happy memories. None of that had changed because she'd stayed in Storm. "Your dad and Chase used to play really well together."

"When I was little, I remember Daddy playing in the living room while I sprawled on my stomach with a coloring book. And sometimes I sang along with him." She placed her hand over her cheek as she chuckled. "Badly, I might add."

"It couldn't have been that bad. I've heard you sing a time or two. You're good enough to have gone on the road with your daddy," Rita Mae said.

"Not everyone is meant for that kind of life," Anna Mae said.

Rita Mae sighed quietly and turned toward the coffee pot. "No, I guess not. So, Mary Louise won't be home for dinner. I guess that means you and I can go out, Anna Mae."

Anna Mae shook her head slightly. "I have a lot of things to do here."

"Hey, that sounds like a great idea," Mary Louise said. "If things change then I'll meet you there."

A wide smile split Rita Mae's face. "Perfect."

"I can't," Anna Mae insisted, rubbing her head as if she had a headache.

"Oh, come on. It'll be fun. We haven't had a meal and a drink at Murphy's Pub in a long time. It'll be nice to—"

"I don't want to go! Not everyone has time to sit around drinking at Murphy's." Anna Mae launched herself to her feet so fast that her chair tilted back and nearly fell over. At the shocked expression on Mary Louise's face, Anna Mae sat back down slowly. "I'm sorry. I…"

"Just because Chase Johnson is back in town, doesn't mean you're going to run into him every time you leave the house. Ever since you ran into him at the barbeque you've been finding busy work. And to be honest, you're becoming a big pain in my ass."

"Rita Mae! In front of Mary Louise?"

Mary Louise laughed. "I'm not ten years old. I've spent a few nights having drinks with friends down at the pub, Anna Mae. It's nothing I haven't heard." Pulling her purse strap up on her shoulder, she headed for the door and called over her shoulder, "Call me on my cell if you end up going to Murphy's. I may stop by."

When she was gone, Rita Mae cast Anna Mae a disapproving glare.

"Don't look at me like that. You're the one who cursed in front of our niece."

"Oh, the hell I did. For God's sake, Mary Louise isn't a child. She's a grown woman. I, for one, hope she ties one on and has herself a good time tonight. Hopefully, she *will* meet up with Tate Johnson and who knows. Maybe she won't come home at all."

Shaking her head, Anna Mae sighed. "Do you really think Tate Johnson is a good match for Mary Louise?"

"It's not our call. It's hers. I saw the way she looked at him at the barbeque. And Tate and Hannah are no longer a couple, so why not have Mary Louise step in and have something for herself? Tate isn't a bum. He's like his dad. He's a community man and he has political aspirations. She could do a whole lot better with him than our brother did by her when he dropped her on our doorstep."

She couldn't argue the point. Mary Louise had been crushed by the events of her life, and at such a young age.

"This isn't easy for me, Rita Mae."

"Oh, for God's sake, she's a grown woman."

"I'm not talking about Mary Louise. Sure, Tate Johnson is a fine man. So is his father. He was always a good friend to me. Especially after Chase left."

"But now he's back."

"Don't start," Anna Mae warned. "I ran into him at the barbeque. I saw him. It's done. Now it's time to move on."

"And that's it? You're just going to let him off the hook after the way he broke your heart?"

"I acted like a damned fool at the barbeque!" She groaned and looked at the ceiling. "I'm not some lovesick youngster. I had my time for that and it's passed me by. I don't need this at this point in my life. I wish…"

"What?"

"I wish he'd never come back to Storm. Things were fine before he came back."

Her sister's expression was sympathetic. "Well, he did come back to Storm. It's his home. So he's here now. As for you, it's either hide in this house for the rest of your life or deal with having Chase Johnson in town for as long as he stays."

"What if he never leaves?"

Rita Mae let out a belly laugh that filled the kitchen. "Oh, sweetie, men like that don't stay. Hasn't he already proven that? He's only been back a handful of times and he never lingers. He'll catch a whiff of something on the wind and he'll be gone all over again. But that doesn't mean you have to hide. In fact, that's the last thing you should do. So you had your little moment at the barbeque and it caught you off center. Big deal. I say it's time to show the man he didn't break you in two when he left. If you're really over him, as you keep arguing you are, then there is no reason not to go on living life as normal."

Anna Mae cocked her head to one side. "When was the last time we went to Murphy's Pub on a Saturday night?"

"That's beside the point. It's high time we go."

Chapter Three

People were packed wall to wall in Murphy's Pub when Chase walked in at half past eight. An old Johnny Cash song was playing on the jukebox and could barely be heard above the laughter and the chatter of the room. If Chase put his money down, he could easily be drunk by nine o'clock. But tonight, he wasn't going to get that lucky.

The meds he'd been taking since his Parkinson's diagnosis warned not to have alcohol, but after today, he needed at least one drink before going back to the ranch and dealing with his brother.

He wasn't sure how long he was going to be able to hide the truth from Zeke. So far Chase's symptoms weren't easily visible because he'd taken pains to make sure he took his meds on time and he played his guitar regularly. No one had to remind him to do that.

Music therapy was often used to lessen the symptoms of Parkinson's disease. Some patients were able to walk steady and even dance after music therapy. For Chase, music was part of his DNA. He didn't have to remember to listen to music every day. He didn't need to learn how to play an instrument like many Parkinson's patients did. It was just a part of him. As long as he could play guitar, his music would help heal him.

Michael Murphy was standing behind the bar telling a story to a man who was a younger version of himself. Must be a grandson, but for the life of him, he couldn't remember which one. Before

Chase could make it to the only empty stool at the bar, Michael let out a booming laugh that filled the space around him. As soon as his gaze landed on Chase, he stopped laughing and his expression turned to surprise. His blue eyes twinkled with pride. Chase guessed it came from living a happy life surrounded by family.

"Well, if it isn't Chase Johnson back from the music city. I heard you were in town. How come it's taken you so long to stop by and see me, son?"

Michael's thick Irish brogue was still evident even after decades of living in Texas. It surprised Chase just how much he missed the sound of it, and the smell and atmosphere of Murphy's.

"I'm due for a good lashing for that, Michael. No excuse other than just getting myself acclimated again. But it's good to finally see you," Chase said, claiming the recently vacated barstool. "How've you been?"

The older man leaned across the bar to shake Chase's hand. His hand was weathered from age and the dark hair that Chase remembered Michael having was now mostly gray. But his old friend looked the same as he had back when Chase and Zeke were still close brothers and the best of friends. Back then, he and Zeke used to frequent Murphy's nearly every evening Chase didn't have a gig.

"I'm still here. That's saying something. It's been a while but you remember my grandson, Logan. He's a war hero, but even more than that, he's my hero." Michael's pride was so strong it was impossible to ignore.

Logan rolled his eyes at Michael. "Gramps, please. Why don't you just put a neon sign in the window?"

Michael laughed. "That's a hell of an idea. I think I will."

Chase extended his hand and shook Logan's. "Actually, I think we talked at the barbeque the other day."

"Yes, we did. Good to see you again," Logan said. "You played a great tune on that guitar. It was amazing."

"Thank you. Do you play?"

Logan looked surprised. "Me? No." He lifted his right hand to show his pinky finger, which was a little crooked. "Thanks to this I don't think I could."

"Are you left or right handed?"

"Right."

"You can do a lot without a pinky finger on the guitar if you're playing right handed. I knew a guy in Nashville with only three fingers on his right hand. He put me to shame."

"After hearing you play, I find that hard to believe. What can I get you?"

What he wanted was a tall glass of whiskey to melt away the unsettled feeling he'd had since seeing his Annie last week at the barbeque. He'd hoped that seeing her would give them both some closure from the past. But that hadn't happened and he realized he was a bigger fool for thinking time had taken care of a lot of the things that hadn't been said years ago. It hadn't.

But despite wanting to drown himself in a glass of whiskey, Chase knew it would interfere with his medication. To keep his secret from his brother and Alice, he'd need to keep that in mind.

"A beer would be good."

"Any particular?"

Chase smiled and looked at Logan. "Give me your best."

Logan tapped the bar top with his fingers. "Sure thing, Chase."

To Michael, Chase said, "You've got a full house tonight already."

"Usually is on a Saturday night. There's not much to do around here so most everyone wanting company ends up at Murphy's."

"Same as always."

"That's the way I like it."

Someone from across the room caught Michael's attention. He waved to whoever it was on the other side of the room and then said, "Excuse me. I have to see about a pretty girl."

Logan dropped a napkin in front of Chase and then placed his beer on top. Chase put a twenty down on the bar to pay for the drink and took a sip of his beer. By the time he put the glass down again, Logan was back with his change, which he placed on the bar next to the beer.

The person on the stool next to him vacated the seat and dropped a tip on the bar. He waved to Logan when he left.

"Thanks!" Logan said, then turned back to Chase. "If you want something to eat, the kitchen is still open. I can get Dad to make you a sandwich or something."

He lifted his hand and shook his head. "This is fine."

Then Logan disappeared to the other end of the bar where there was a lot of noise and laughter.

Another song came on over the jukebox. Chase could barely hear it over the laughter and chatter around him. He loved the sound. Always had. It was second only to the feeling of being on stage and it made the lonely feeling of going home to an empty bed a little more tolerable.

He felt a hand on his shoulder and turned to see his nephew Tate behind him.

"How far ahead of me are you?" he asked Chase.

Chase picked up the beer and said, "First one."

"I don't have far to go to catch up to you then." Tate slid onto the empty stool and raised his hand, peering down the length of the bar to get Logan's attention.

"Logan's filling in for Uncle Aidan, I see," Tate said. "I wonder what's up with that?"

"He said his dad is back in the kitchen."

Tate chuckled. "The kitchen? Not to sound sexist but that's best left to Aunt Sonya, unless Uncle Aidan is making a roast beef sandwich."

Logan appeared in front of them. "What'll you have?"

"Same as Chase."

"Sure thing."

"Ever since he broke up with Ginny Moreno, Logan's looked a bit lost," Tate said, watching his young cousin work the bar.

"He seems pretty quick on his feet here."

"You didn't see him when he returned from Afghanistan."

Chase took a sip of his beer. "I'm sure that was rough."

Tate looked around the room quickly.

"Meeting someone?" Chase asked.

"Maybe."

"Would that someone be a girl named Hannah?"

Tate gave him a sidelong glance as Logan set down his beer. Chase took a ten-dollar bill from the change Logan had given him earlier to pay for his nephew's beer. Tate then lifted his glass of beer and gestured a thank you to Chase before taking a sip.

"What do you know about Hannah Grossman?" Tate asked.

"Well, it's been a long time, but I know the family. I know she's a pretty girl. And I know that the two of you were an item for a time."

His jaw clenched. "We still would be if Tucker hadn't seduced her."

"Ah, so that's the reason for the chill at dinner the other night."

"It's best you stay out of this, Uncle Chase. It's between Tucker and me."

"True enough. But what about Hannah? She was part of it too. Seems to me she couldn't have been taken by Tucker against her will."

"I really don't want to talk about this," Tate said.

"Okay, fine. So I'm guessing you're not here to see Hannah. So who is it?"

"I was supposed to meet with Mary Louise Prager this afternoon but I got caught in a meeting so I told her I'd meet her here for a drink."

"Mary Louise Prager. Is that George Prager's little girl?"

Tate smiled. "She's no little girl anymore. We weren't all caught in a time warp while you were away."

He shrugged. "I suppose not."

But it sure felt that way to Chase. The lines on his face showed he'd aged, but in his mind Anna Mae had stayed as young and beautiful as she was the day he'd left her. After seeing her at the barbeque, he knew she was still as beautiful. But life had taken away some of that spark.

Michael had returned to the back of the bar and now he stopped in front of Tate and Chase.

"Are you talking about Mary Louise?" Michael asked. "I was just talking to her. She mentioned she might meet you here, Tate. She's over there with her aunts."

Both Tate and Chase turned in the direction Michael was pointing. Chase couldn't believe that he hadn't seen Anna Mae when he'd walked into Murphy's. She had to have been here when he'd arrived. There was no way he could have missed her coming through the door.

Tate picked up his beer and slid off the stool. "I'm going to go say hello to Mary Louise. Good to see you, Uncle Chase."

He looked in the direction Michael pointed. He couldn't see the back table given the movement of people in the room. But he knew where to go.

"I think I'll join you, if you don't mind."

Chapter Four

They made their way through the crowd to a booth in the back near the tiny stage. Chase felt a tug in his chest when he saw the small spotlight shining on the chair and empty music stand. That was his place. That's where he felt most like himself. But not tonight.

"You were hiding from me," Tate said when he reached the table where Mary Louise and her aunts were sitting. The smile on Annie's face collapsed when she saw Chase.

She might not be happy to see him, but he didn't share that feeling. It surprised him just how much he'd wanted to see Annie again.

They both were a lot older than they'd been when they'd been lovers years ago. Her blonde hair had turned to gray and the long curly locks she used to wear hanging down to the middle of her back were gone. Her hair was short now, making her curls even tighter. Her eyes were still that gray blue that had driven him wild as a young buck and her laugh, well, that had always been his undoing.

But she wasn't laughing or smiling now. She climbed out of the booth and stalked over to the jukebox before he could utter a word.

"Sorry about that," Mary Louise said with an embarrassed shrug.

"Why? You didn't do anything," Chase said. "It's good to see you again. And you too, Rita Mae."

Rita Mae's smile was tight. "Tate, why don't you have a seat?"

He would have laughed at the way Rita Mae was blowing him

off, but he didn't want to sit anyway.

"I have to see about a girl," Chase said.

He didn't wait to hear Rita Mae's protest. Instead, Chase made his way through the crowd in the direction where Annie had disappeared. He found her over by the jukebox looking at the songs. She gave no indication that she'd heard his approach. However, when he was finally standing behind her, she glanced up at him and didn't seem surprised at all that he'd followed her.

"Find anything good?"

"What are you doing here?" she asked. Gone was the anger she'd had last week at the barbeque when they'd talked briefly.

"Same thing you are. Looking for a dance partner."

She laughed cynically. "You flatter yourself."

"You're as beautiful as you were before I left for Nashville."

He'd meant the compliment, but her stricken expression made him question voicing his thoughts out loud to her.

"Don't say things you don't mean."

"Since when have I not meant that?"

"I wouldn't know. It's been a long time and I'm sure a whole lot of women between then and now."

One of the things Chase had always loved about Annie was that despite the fact that he dwarfed her small stature, she had a spitfire personality that hadn't changed over the years. She turned to walk around him but he caught her by the arm. She glanced at his hand but didn't pull away.

"There's never been anyone like you, Annie. I wouldn't lie about something like that."

Her bottom lip trembled. Chase longed to brush his thumb across it and then follow with a kiss.

"Don't do that," she whispered.

"Do what? I have no illusion that I can change the past. But I don't want you thinking I left here for something that wasn't true. It wasn't other women. I'm not going to say that I was a saint because I'd be lying."

"I don't want to hear it," she said, shifting her feet and looking away.

"Don't do that."

"You have no right to tell me what to do. You're the one who left me."

"You didn't stop me. You told me to go."

She paused for a second and then took a deep breath. "Yes, I did. I didn't want you to resent me for wanting you to stay."

"I could never resent you."

She shook her head and her curls bounced, making her look like a young woman again.

"You say that now. But I know what it's like to give up on dreams. I did that, remember? If my parents hadn't died the way they did and Rita Mae…well, I probably would have stayed in New York and…"

He finished her sentence for her. "We never would have fallen in love. I hope that's not something you regret. Because I don't."

The song that Annie had chosen on the jukebox started to play. It was an old Temptations song they used to dance to. By the look on her face, she was lost in that memory.

"I don't want to talk about this, Chase."

"Dance with me."

Her eyes widened. "Here?"

He took her by her hands and started swinging to the music. "Why not?"

"Are you crazy?"

"Yes. But that's beside the point."

She straightened her back and pulled her hands from his. "I don't want to dance. I have to go."

She took off through the crowd and Chase didn't follow her. It was just as well. The music was being eclipsed by the noise in the room and wasn't having the healing effect it always had. Dancing was good therapy for Parkinson's patients. But he wasn't thinking about therapy. He was thinking of his Annie being in his arms.

But not in the condition he was in now. As the moments went on, he felt the trembling in his left leg and his hands increase. When he danced with Annie again, if he ever had that pleasure to dance with her again, he didn't want her to see a broken down old man. He wanted her to see him like he saw her. Young and full of life. Beautiful.

He shoved his hands in his pockets and slowly made his way through the bar.

"Uncle Chase?" Tate called out to him. But Chase ignored him. He kept walking because as much as noise and confusion and music had been part of his whole life, both here and in Nashville, he could feel the man he was slipping away.

* * * *

"You're here bright and early this morning," Hedda Garten said as Marylee and her beautiful granddaughter Brittany walked into the flower shop. "Are you here for a special occasion or just for a splash of color in the house?"

Marylee's trip to the flower shop had been for a reason, but it hadn't been for the sole purpose of purchasing flowers. Ever since the disastrous events on the square, Brittany had been in need of some attention. The humiliation caused by the scandal of having her best friend and her father's affair front and center on everyone's mind made her cling to her relationship with Marcus Alvarez. It was high time Marylee intervened. Enough was enough, and Brittany could certainly do better. She was a Rush, after all.

While at Probst Pharmacy the other day, she'd heard from Kristin Douglas that Hedda Garten's great-grandson and a handsome young friend were visiting Storm. It was just the distraction Brittany needed.

"Every house needs some daisies. Don't you think, Brittany?"

Brittany looked around the shop but seemed uninterested in anything Marylee had to say.

"Brittany? Did you find anything, dear?"

"I don't know what you want, Grams."

"You have an opinion about so many other things, just give me your opinion on which flowers to choose."

"I ordered some new exotic flowers and had my great-grandson pick them up from the flower market this morning," Hedda said. "He's in the back room unpacking them with his friend Scott now. Would you like to see those?"

"Oh, do ask them to bring the flowers out here. I'd heard your great-grandson was visiting. I'd love to meet him," Marylee said.

Brittany rolled her eyes and went to the cooler where Hedda kept the ready-made arrangements. Hedda went into the back room. Marylee could hear talking, but couldn't make out the words. A few minutes later, two young men came out front. Each of them held a box of flowers.

"Marylee. Brittany. You both know my great-grandson, Max, and his friend Scott Wallace. Don't you?"

Marylee looked at both of the boys. They both looked to be about the same age as Brittany.

"Yes, we do. Max and I went to college together," Brittany said.

"Hello, ma'am," Max said.

Brittany smiled. "Max, why didn't you text me you were coming to town?"

"Just got here. I let Ginny know. I thought for sure she would have told you."

Marylee cleared her throat. "I do believe we might have met at Jacob Salt's funeral? Is that right? I'd forgotten you were Jacob's roommate." Marylee pushed aside her disappointment; after all, there was still another young man. And that meant another chance of distracting Brittany.

"I haven't had a chance to see Ginny yet," Max said to Brittany. "How is she doing?"

Brittany blanched. "She's fine, I guess. We don't really talk much anymore."

Max had the good sense to look embarrassed. Anger filled Marylee. Did that girl know everyone on the planet?

"What about you, Scott?" she asked, before the conversation strayed too far. "Do you go to UT, too?"

Scott shook his head. "I grew up with Max. But I go to A&M."

"Really? That's impressive."

Brittany rolled her eyes, which earned a smile from Scott.

"A&M's football program has gotten a lot stronger," Brittany said.

Scott seemed surprised. "You like football?"

Brittany giggled. "I go to UT. Not much of a choice, really."

Marylee watched the interaction between Brittany and Scott. He was a handsome young man, and A&M certainly wasn't some small-town college. Though he wasn't exactly perfect for Brittany either, he might do as a distraction for now.

"The two of you should stop by the house tomorrow for lunch. You can introduce Jeffry to Scott and maybe the four of you could do something together."

"Grams, what are you doing?"

Hedda's smile was instantaneous. "That's a fabulous idea."

"I'd love to stop by," Scott said. "I've never been to this part of Texas. Maybe you could give us a tour."

Brittany was clearly not happy with her, but Marylee didn't care. If giving the boys a tour of the area kept Brittany away from Marcus Alvarez, then it was worth Brittany being a little angry with her.

Feeling satisfied that she'd accomplished her goal, Marylee said, "I'll take the daisies, Hedda."

* * * *

This picture was a good one. With a shaky hand, Celeste picked up the stick of glue and dabbed it on the blank scrapbook page before pressing the photo of Jacob onto the paper. He was happy. Such a beautiful, happy child.

She searched the pile of snapshots she'd pulled out of the boxes they'd tucked in the attic the last time they'd painted the walls in their house. Somehow the images of when the children were little had stayed there. But today Celeste had been ready to unearth them again.

Sniffing back tears, she chose another baby picture. This time it was a shot of Jacob as a toddler. He'd been so good. So happy. He'd never given her an ounce of trouble.

The photo had been taken at the dining room table where Celeste was sitting now. He'd been holding onto one of the chairs and smiling up at her as she snapped the photo. It was as if Jacob were actually there in the room with her again.

She dabbed the glue on the scrapbook page. It wasn't fair.

None of it. Her Jacob was gone and now… She had nothing.

Anger swirled through her as she thought of the lies Ginny Moreno had fed her. Fed them all. Nothing could be crueler than pretending to be carrying the baby of the child Celeste had lost. The child Ginny had stolen from her with her reckless driving in that car accident. And now she'd stolen two children. Except the grandchild Celeste had thought she'd celebrate running on the floors of this house, just like Jacob had, was only fiction.

She pasted the picture. Then another. Then she got up from the dining room table and poured herself a tall glass of vodka before returning to her task.

"Here's another one," she whispered, trembling with the vodka glass at her lips.

Celeste picked up the photo and looked at it through tear-filled eyes. It was the day they'd taken Lacey home from the hospital and Jacob met his baby sister for the first time. As a toddler, Jacob looked lost in the chair that he'd eventually filled out nicely as a teenager. He'd held Lacey and looked at her so seriously. Celeste's arms were barely visible in the photo as she supported his chubby body, sagging with the weight of the baby as Travis took the picture.

"What are you doing?"

Celeste snapped her gaze up and saw Lacey standing in the doorway. Sniffing back tears, she said, "I didn't know you were home."

"You don't notice me much these days."

Celeste felt her bottom lip tremble. By the stricken look on Lacey's face, she knew her daughter regretted her words.

"I didn't mean that."

"Yes, you did," she said delicately. "And I can't blame you. I haven't been myself. I don't think I ever will be again."

Chapter Five

He'd spent an hour playing his guitar as soon as he'd woken up. Normally Chase would have had a cup of coffee and a shower before doing anything. But music helped his body wake up more than caffeine did these days. Music was as much his medicine as the scripts his doctor wrote for him.

Now showered and feeling more himself, Chase left his bedroom and headed downstairs for some breakfast.

"Dinner is at six every night," Zeke said, as Chase descended the staircase.

Chase met his brother at the bottom of the landing before speaking. "Is that right?"

"Don't play with me, Chase. The people who help run this house may not be kin, but they are family. Some of them have been with us since just after you left Storm. To that end, nothing has changed here since the last time you lived here."

Chase's eyebrows stretched on his forehead. "I can think of a whole lot of things that have changed. You weren't married then. Back then you were sweet on my girl."

His jaw tightened. "Your girl? Too bad you forgot that when you left here. But let me remind you of this. Our father was running this ranch back then, too, and it broke his heart that you left and never came home. We could have used your help. Instead, you strapped that damned guitar on your back and left Storm and any responsibility you had here."

"I seem to remember you giving me a black eye as payment. It was quite the talk on my first day in the studio."

Zeke shook his head and balled his fist. Chase had a feeling his brother had been itching to give Chase another black eye for some time. But Zeke held his temper, something he must have learned over the years. Or maybe Alice had mellowed him some.

Alice was a good match for his brother. He'd barely known her before he left Storm, but in the short time he'd been back at the ranch, he saw how much his brother's wife complemented him. Chase was genuinely happy for his brother, for the life he'd built here while he was gone. Aside from Chase's presence on the ranch, Zeke seemed happy.

"We still have staff that work here and we respect the job they do on our behalf," Zeke said. "I know you're not of a mind to think of anyone other than yourself, but if you're not going to be home for dinner, I'd appreciate you telling the staff so you don't waste their time."

"The cooks here have always prepared enough for an army. There's never been a problem with having extra at the dinner table. I really didn't think there'd be a problem with one less." He hadn't even thought of it, which only proved Zeke's point that Chase had been thoughtless. "I guess it's too much of a burden to take a plate off the table? Or was it staring at the empty chair that you had a hard time with?"

Zeke's face turned red. "You really don't give a damn about anyone, do you?"

"I was at Murphy's last night having a drink with Tate. You haven't seen him since that awkward family dinner we had the other night, I take it."

Zeke's surprise was evident in the way he pulled back from his anger. But he recovered quickly.

"Tate is a grown man. He goes about his business as he sees fit. I don't keep up on all he does. But when it comes to this ranch, I do. If you're living here, then you need to abide by how things are done here. This ranch has always been run tight, Chase. I don't know or care about the kind of reckless life you led in Nashville, but there are still rules here and we still respect the people who work for us to make our lives easier. We don't take them for granted. If Daddy were alive today he'd have you out in back of the barn whipping your hide for your behavior."

"I think we're both a long way from getting a whipping." At Zeke's cold glare, Chase amended, "It's been a while. I forgot how Mom always ran the household with a strict hand. I guess Alice does that too? I'll remember to call next time."

"See that you do."

Zeke propped his Stetson on his head and headed for the kitchen. Chase waited until he heard the kitchen door open and shut before heading into the kitchen himself. Okay, that made him a coward and he'd never been a coward where his brother was concerned. But he didn't have the want or the need for a fight this morning. Pretty soon, he wouldn't have the strength.

The kitchen was empty when he walked inside. The red light on the coffee pot was still lit and the pot was half full. He opened the cabinet and grabbed a mug before placing it on the granite counter. After pouring a cup of coffee, he took a sip as he walked over to the breakfast table by the window and winced at the bitter taste. The coffee was still hot but it had been sitting too long.

Pulling a chair away from the table, he sat down. He'd drink the coffee anyway because he needed it. Taking another sip, he glanced through the white eyelet curtains in the direction of the barn. Tucker and a young woman wearing a well-worn pair of jeans and her hair tied back in a braid were walking out of the barn arm in arm. Both of them were laughing about something.

"Must be the famous Hannah," he mumbled.

Women. Wars were waged for them. At least between friends and family. This time it was brothers. He didn't know all the details. He'd only just heard rumors at the barbeque. But he did know that Hannah had once been his nephew Tate's girl, something Tate had acknowledged himself. And from the looks of the way Hannah and Tucker embraced openly under the hot sun, things had surely changed.

Hannah climbed into her truck and pulled out of the parking area, waving to Tucker while he waited on the grass. She was a pretty girl, much like her mother had been at that age. She had an easy way about her that was hard to ignore.

He glanced over at Tucker. Even from where he was sitting, Chase recognized a man in love.

"Shit," he mumbled and then drained his mug.

Chase didn't need to know the details. He could figure out most of what was relevant himself. But he did know that whatever had gone down had created a rift between Tate and Tucker that was beginning to look like what happened between him and Zeke. And he didn't much like that at all.

* * * *

Fifteen minutes later, Chase walked out to the paddock where Tucker was now working with Pringles, one of the horses. When Chase was sitting at the breakfast table, he'd seen Zeke with his two grandchildren, Carol Ann and Danny, riding the horses.

Chase has seen his brother's grandchildren before at the barbeque. The little one, Danny, was a handful and everyone at the barbeque had an eye on him at all times. The boy's father, a pastor at the local church, had mentioned that Danny had autism. Chase didn't know anything about autism, but he did know love and that boy was the apple of Bryce Douglas's eye just like his big sister Carol.

Chase headed out to the barn only after he'd seen Zeke take the children into the house, leaving Tucker to tend to the horses. When Chase and Zeke were kids, leaving a horse without tending to its needs was cause for a whipping. You never left a horse without making sure it was rubbed down and watered after a ride. But what did Chase know about raising young ones or spoiling by a grandparent? The only person he'd had to care for was himself.

Tucker glanced up from undoing the cinch on Pringles' saddle when he approached.

"You up for a ride, Uncle Chase? I can get one of the other horses."

Chase shook his head and rubbed the horse's neck. A ride would be nice, but the heat was already enough to melt him into the ground. Besides, he had other things on his mind.

"I noticed things were a little chilly at the dinner table the other night. You and Tate weren't exactly cordial to each other."

Tucker paused for a second, and then continued his task before pulling the saddle off Carol's horse.

"Didn't think it would bother you so much. You and Dad have barely spoken two words to each other since you arrived in Storm. At least in my presence."

"Fair enough. But Zeke and I, we have a history that goes way back before you were born, son. Time doesn't always heal bad blood. Sometimes it makes it worse."

"This isn't like you and my father."

Chase wasn't so sure of that. There were deeper issues that had driven him and Zeke apart, but it had all started with a woman.

Tucker handed him the saddle. The weight of it, despite the fact that it was a child's saddle, left him momentarily unsteady on his feet.

"You got that?" he asked.

Chase gripped the saddle. "It's fine. What's not fine is what's happening with you and Tate. No woman is worth causing a divide between brothers."

Tucker's expression was one of surprise. It wasn't Chase's place to drag out old arguments that had been secret between him and Zeke for so long. Especially if his kids had no clue about their father's past. It had been left there where secrets should stay buried. And they would have if Chase had stayed in Nashville and forgotten that he and Zeke had once been close friends as well as brothers, and he'd once had the love of a woman like Anna Mae Prager.

"Who says what's between us is about a woman? Honestly, Uncle Chase, it's probably best you don't get in the middle of things with me and Tate."

"I live here. It's hard not to."

Tucker didn't bother meeting his gaze.

"Of course it's over a woman," Chase said, laughing. "It's always over a woman."

"I'm not a damned country song," Tucker said as he took the bridle off the horse.

"No? Could have fooled me. Young buck steals his brother's

girl and leaves him with nothing but heartache? Sounds like something I've heard on the radio before."

Tucker grabbed the blanket from the horse's back and started walking toward the barn, then stopped and turned to look at Chase. "You going to hold that saddle all day or put it back in the tack room?"

"Wasn't sure if I was welcome." That earned him a quick smile from his nephew. Tucker was a lot like him. He hadn't had the pleasure of bonding with his brother's kids while they were growing up. But seeing Tucker as the man he'd become reminded Chase of what it was like to be young and full of passion. Tucker had that passion for ranching the way Chase had it for music. And for Annie.

"Sure, you let the old man carry the saddle while you carry a blanket?" he said with a low chuckle.

Tucker flashed a quick smile. "I'm not stupid."

He followed Tucker into the barn and returned the saddle to the empty spot next to the rest of the saddles.

"You don't look like the political type," Chase said.

"Beg your pardon?"

"You're a cowboy," Chase said. "It's clear you're more at home here than in a suit and tie like Tate."

"So?"

He shrugged. "Just that I'm having a hard time figuring where this bad blood is coming from. You don't follow your brother's political aspirations. So my guess is it's about that pretty girl I saw you with earlier." He grinned. "Like I said, it's about a woman."

Tucker grabbed a pail and propped it under the faucet before turning the water on. "I think you think too much."

"You know when I left here all those years ago, your father wasn't too happy with me. Some of that unhappiness is still in him. I left him with a load of work on this ranch and all the responsibility to keep it solvent."

"The ranch runs just fine."

"That's what I'm saying. It runs this way because of what Zeke put into it. What he taught you. And it continues to run because of the love and care you put in it."

Tucker turned off the water when the pail was full. "What's your point?"

"I left for my dream. My passion. It pissed your old man off and because of that we spent a lot of years not speaking to each other. Only now when I look at you I see that same thing brewing between you and your brother. That girl Hannah, she doesn't seem so much like the type of woman Tate would be interested in given his political goals."

"She's a veterinarian. She loves animals. Loves being out on the ranch."

"Not the type to hold fancy parties just to impress a bunch of uptight people that can further Tate's political career?"

Tucker chuckled. "Are you saying my dad is uptight? He *has* been the mayor of Storm for a long time."

"I think your mom keeps him grounded just like this ranch does."

Tucker nodded and gave him a warm smile. "I think you're right about that."

"See, the thing is, I'd hate to see years go by before you get to the bottom of whatever it is that's really causing this distance between you and Tate. If it's this woman and you really care for her, then you need to get it all out in the open and eventually he'll accept it. If she's just some passing fancy, it's not worth her driving a wedge between you and your brother."

Tucker glanced up at him uncomfortably, then grabbed the pail of water. "It's not a passing fancy. What's happened can't be undone, Uncle Chase. It may not have happened the way it should have, but it is what it is."

"Tucker?"

The deep voice that boomed in the open aisle of the barn told Chase that Zeke was none too happy.

"Back here, Dad," Tucker said. He glanced at his father and took in the cold glare he was giving Chase. Tucker looked at Chase and then his dad. "I need to bring Pringles in."

"Then get to it," Zeke said.

Tucker walked out of the barn holding the bucket of water.

"You all of a sudden have an interest in fixing my family's

problems as if you know anything at all about them?" Zeke said, his jaw clenched tight as if his teeth would break under the pressure.

"Fixing?"

"You may share his blood but you're still a stranger to that boy, Chase," Zeke said. "You haven't been with him every day of his entire life. I don't need you walking into his life and shaking things up any more than they already are."

Chase couldn't argue that point. His sole contribution to his niece's and nephew's lives had been Christmas and birthday presents.

"He's still my nephew. He's family."

Zeke shook his head just enough to show his disgust. "You don't exactly have a good track record with family."

"What you're really saying is I have no record at all. No wife. No children. Isn't that right?"

Zeke cast him a cold glare that bothered Chase more than it should have because it was deserved.

"I have no idea what your life was like back in Nashville, Chase. Quite frankly, I couldn't care less. The music world is as foreign to me as having tea and crumpets at a Sunday social. Your escapades are your own business. But what's happened here in this family, on this ranch, is my business. You have no right giving my son advice about something you know nothing about."

"And what's that?"

"Family."

"I never stopped being family. Nashville didn't change that."

"How about loyalty? Responsibility? Is any of that something you know about? You know, you didn't exactly leave a smile on the faces of the people who cared about you when you left. Some people had to carry the burdens you left behind."

"I've never been a rancher, Zeke."

"That's true enough. There are no accolades securing barbed wire to fences in Texas. The cattle don't care much about the songs you're playing on the guitar. But people here sure do care. This family cares. And you left."

"Just like Tate?"

Zeke cast him a sidelong glance. "My son went to college. He became a respected lawyer and made something of himself here in Storm. That's a lot more than you ever did. Stay away from my sons, Chase."

He started to walk away, but then turned around.

"What makes you think you can come back to Storm and step in like you never left? What the hell kind of life experience do you have to offer them for their troubles? You have no children of your own. No life mate. The only woman who was worth loving is the one you tossed aside for fame and fortune. You left her, Chase. And then you never looked back. I had to pick up the pieces of the debris you left behind. You have lived a life with no responsibility. No one to sacrifice anything for." Zeke waved his arms with anger and his eyes flared with fire he could barely control. "You're staying on this ranch because this was our father's home and I can't turn you out. But I can tell you this. Stay away from my children. I've spent a lifetime raising them and loving them. I don't need you fouling up their lives with your fool advice."

Zeke turned and walked out of the barn without another word. Chase had deserved every bit of anger his brother gave him. Chase had left home, leaving Zeke to make things right. Debris? He didn't know exactly what that was all about. But he couldn't deny there was a whole lot of hurt with his family and Annie when he'd left.

One of the horses whinnied and bobbed his head over the door of his stall as if he'd been distressed by the tension he'd witnessed. Chase sighed as he walked over to the animal, rubbing his neck until he calmed. If only it were that easy to calm the fury he'd caused with the people in his life.

Chapter Six

The produce looked old, Anna Mae thought as she picked up a head of romaine lettuce and inspected it. Why Rita Mae insisted she come to this market to buy their produce for the bed and breakfast was beyond her. She put the lettuce back in place and moved the shopping cart down to check the peppers, then the radicchio. Nothing looked appealing enough for her to want to buy here.

"You have too pretty a face to look that disgusted, Annie."

It amazed Anna Mae that she recognized Chase's voice so quickly, even though it had been years since she'd heard it on a regular basis. That Texas drawl should have diminished some over the decades he'd been in Nashville, but she still heard it as if Chase Johnson hadn't left Storm at all.

Bracing herself with her hands gripped tightly to the shopping cart, she glanced up to see the blue eyes that had haunted her dreams for years. Ever since he'd returned to Storm, she couldn't get the image of the young man she'd loved out of her mind. Neither one of them were young like that now. But even though his hair had turned gray and his face was weathered with age, his eyes were still that same deep blue and he was as handsome as he was the day he'd left Storm.

"Not disgusted. Just disappointed," she said, trying to focus on the produce instead of Chase's face.

"I'm not sure I like that."

Her eyes widened as she glanced at him quickly. "You'd rather me be disgusted?"

"I'd rather you be smiling. I like that a lot better."

She pulled in a deep breath as bitterness filled her. Would that ever go away? "Really? You should have seen me after you left for Nashville."

It was a cheap shot. After all this time Anna Mae hadn't realized she was capable of firing off such venom. She'd thought she'd gotten out all her anger and heartache over Chase years ago.

Chase knew nothing about her hard days after he'd left for Nashville. Not just because she missed him, although that alone had brought her to her knees many times. But when she'd lost the baby she was carrying, she grieved alone. She'd never told Chase about the baby. She wanted him to come home to her, not out of obligation. And when the baby who'd comforted her throughout her grieving for the man she loved died in her womb, her entire world shattered. She couldn't tell Chase about the baby then. He hadn't come home to her and he would surely resent her for not allowing him to be a part of what little time their child had existed in this world, even if it was only in her womb.

Anna Mae had shut Chase out. It had been her decision pure and simple. She'd chosen to deal with it all on her own. Which wasn't really fair. Her grief had turned to anger over the years, but it wasn't his fault. Not for that anyway.

A wave of regret washed over her. Her words had affected him. That much was evident from the way his expression collapsed.

She didn't want to feel guilty for her cheap shot, but she did.

"Are you going to follow me around the store all day or are you here to shop?"

Chase moved close enough to her so she could feel the heat of his body. The store wasn't quiet. There were children running down a few aisles away and a young mother telling them to behave. A stock boy was clumsily stacking cans on a shelf not far from them. And the sound of the produce cooler's motor hummed loud enough to hear. But Anna Mae could swear she could hear the thump of Chase's heartbeat.

Or maybe it was a memory. She had a lot of those. Some wonderful. Some not so good. Some so heartbreaking that she didn't want to remember. But his heart beating next to her ear when she laid her head on his chest after they'd made love was a memory that had stayed with her. She couldn't possibly be hearing his heartbeat now. But the rise and fall of his chest beneath the dusty blue cotton shirt he wore brought it all back.

"Annie." The deep timbre of Chase's voice caught her off guard, and her cheeks flamed. He'd caught her in the memory. But if he knew what she'd been thinking, the smile on his face didn't show it. Instead, his smile was warm and his blue-eyed gaze penetrated her until her whole body tingled.

It had been a long time since Anna Mae had experienced feelings like this. The last time she had, she'd been with Chase.

"I have to finish shopping so I can get dinner started, Chase. I have guests who expect me to feed them."

"I thought you just served breakfast."

"Did you check up on me?"

"I asked about the bed and breakfast."

Disappointment filled her when normally having someone asking about the business she'd built with her sister would give her pride. But Anna Mae foolishly thought for a split second that maybe Chase had asked specifically about her.

"You don't want me asking around?"

"Well, of course you can," Anna Mae said, gripping the handle of the shopping cart and moving it a few feet. "Most people around Storm know our reputation. We get a lot of business from people who come to town and ask around for places to stay. I assume the people you asked had good things to say?"

She picked up a cantaloupe. She wasn't going to buy it but she needed something to do with her hands so he wouldn't see how rattled she was.

"All glowing praise. You've done well for yourself, Anna Mae."

She liked his praise but it came with a cost to her heart. Her chest tightened. She placed her hand over her chest where she felt the squeeze.

"I didn't do it alone," she said quietly. "I had my sister. And then of course when Mary Louise got older she helped a lot too."

His eyebrows lifted. "Are you going to buy that cantaloupe or just hold it until it's good and ripe?"

She chuckled and put the piece of fruit back on the pile. "Contemplating."

"Ah."

"To answer your question, yes, we just serve breakfast. But I need to eat too, and so does the rest of my family. I love to cook."

"I remember that about you."

Her mouth dropped open just enough to show her surprise. "You do?"

He leaned forward. "Anna Mae Prager, I remember every single detail about you." He drew in a short breath and let it out slowly. "I always have."

Emotion bubbled inside her and rose up her throat. She didn't know if she could trust opening her mouth to speak.

She should be angry with Chase for all the nights she'd been alone crying for him. And for their baby. But she had no right. She'd given him her blessing to leave, albeit reluctantly. What woman wants to let go of a man like Chase Johnson?

But she wasn't going to be responsible for keeping him in Storm. Some men were meant to dig in roots. Some were gypsies, just like the gypsy ladies they sang about in country songs.

But that wasn't her. She wouldn't have lasted a week on the road living like that. Sure, she'd wanted excitement when she'd gone to New York City. She'd loved being there. But even in New York, she'd been grounded. She'd had a small apartment and a job in a restaurant. It wasn't quite what she'd expected when she'd gone to New York. But she always knew that if she worked hard, she'd be happy there.

But then Rita Mae had needed her. She'd come home to help her sister deal with the loss of their parents as well as the far-too-early death in Vietnam of the man Rita Mae had dearly loved. It didn't seem right to return to New York after that. And then she'd met and fallen in love with Chase. And when he'd left, Rita Mae was still so broken. How could she have followed Chase when that would have meant leaving Rita Mae all alone?

"Didn't you come here to buy something?" Anna Mae said, pushing the grocery basket again. She couldn't stand there any longer feeling unnerved by Chase. It was as if everyone in the grocery store knew what she had been thinking, could see what she was feeling. Especially Chase.

He had to know how much Anna Mae had loved him. And she'd known how important it had been for him to go to Nashville and reach for his dream of making it big in music. But even though she'd given Chase her blessing to go, a big part of her hadn't thought he'd leave.

She'd found out she was pregnant after he'd left. But how could she tell him then? He would have come home out of duty, not for her. No, if Chase Johnson was going to return to Storm, Anna Mae wanted it to be because he'd loved her so much he couldn't live without her.

But he'd never come home. And the love they'd had died along with their unborn baby. Anna Mae was too old to look back and have regrets on what might have been if she'd made different decisions. She had to move forward.

"I came to see you," Chase said with a wide smile that melted her heart the way it had the first time she'd seen it when he was a young man and she was a naïve girl.

"How did you even know I'd be here?"

"I stopped by your place."

She blinked. "The bed and breakfast?"

"Yeah. Your sister wasn't there but the kid who mows your lawn told me you'd left for the market. By the way, where is Rita Mae?"

"Ah, she went to a craft fair in Fredericksburg. It's not like we don't have enough crafts to choose from right here in Storm, but she wants to fill up the house and the cafe with more trinkets. Sometimes the guests and diners like to buy souvenirs even if they're not made in Storm."

"Sort of like fine English teacups made in Japan?"

Anna Mae chuckled, but then waved him off. "Something like that. Look, I really have to finish this. Maybe we'll bump into each other again before you leave."

She only managed to push the shopping cart a few feet before she heard his deep voice at her back.

"Don't you even want to know why I was looking for you?"

She did. "No."

"Liar."

A fingernail of irritation scraped up her spine. She turned around slowly. "What did you say to me?"

"You heard me."

"I was hoping I didn't." Anna Mae could hardly contain her anger. *Chase* had the audacity to call *her* a liar?

"You're dying to know why I came to see you, Annie."

"Don't call me that. No one calls me that."

"I've always called you that."

"I know. And I don't want you to."

"You're too stubborn, Annie. You see, I think you secretly like it, but you don't want to admit it. Just like you don't want to admit you really want to know why I came to see you. But you won't ask. You'll wait until I tell you. But I'm not going to."

"How does that make me stubborn?"

"You didn't come with me to Nashville."

"You're the one who left." She was only vaguely aware that her voice has risen and she was still standing in the middle of a crowded grocery store. She looked around and didn't see anyone looking at her.

She tried to pull herself together, acknowledging how much seeing Chase again had thrown her off center. From the first moment she'd seen him in Storm, she'd known she'd have trouble dealing with her residual anger. But she hadn't thought it would shatter her as it had all those years ago. And yet here she was, an absolute wreck.

She sighed. When the hell was he leaving Storm?

"You could have followed me, Annie. I would have liked it if you had."

"Why does any of this matter now after all these years? Look, we've been through this. If you stopped by the B&B to talk, there's nothing for us to say, Chase. I thought I made that clear at the barbeque, and then again last night. Our lives moved on in different directions. We've…spent a lifetime without each other. We don't even know each other anymore. There's nothing left to say."

"Are you done shopping?"

She blinked hard. Hadn't he just heard her? "Chase…"

"I'll help you finish and then I'll help you bring the groceries home."

"What?"

"You heard me. There's nothing wrong with your hearing."

"True, but there's clearly something wrong with yours. I have been shopping for my bed and breakfast for years. I don't need your help and I don't want your help. Now if you'll excuse me, I have things to do."

Turning on her heels, Anna Mae pushed the cart to the middle of the frozen food aisle and then looked around to see if Chase had followed her. She'd run away like a beaten dog with her tail between her legs. Taking in each breath to steady her rampant heartbeat, she realized Rita Mae was right. She hadn't resolved anything after all these years. Decades had been wasted. And still, the only man who could make her blood boil or stir her heart was Chase Johnson.

Damn him.

* * * *

Well, that went well. Chase watched Anna Mae from a distance. It had been a mistake to follow her here thinking she'd actually be happy to see him. What the hell had he turned himself into?

In Nashville he was a much sought after studio musician. Every club manager he talked to booked him for a night at their club because they knew he'd bring a crowd. People loved him.

In Nashville. He hadn't found so much love here in Storm despite all his kin living here.

It was his own fault. You couldn't burn bridges the way he had without needing to later find a way to rebuild them. He had a long way to go if there was any hope of making things right, or as right as they could be with his kin and with Annie.

He didn't blame her for wanting to keep her distance. He'd hurt her when he'd chosen his music over life here in Storm. There was a time during the days before he left that Chase had been convinced she was going to pack her bags and leave with him. But she hadn't. Kin was important to her, and her sister had been dealing with her own pain at the time. Annie hadn't wanted to leave her.

Chase could deal with Zeke's anger toward him a whole lot easier than dealing with Annie's. But she was right. He hadn't called her. He'd walked away and never looked back until now.

Nashville was so different than Storm. Things happened for him quickly once he'd arrived and met a few of the local musicians playing in the clubs. He'd been busy. He'd had his reasons for not calling her. But most of all, Chase knew that the sweet sound of Annie's voice and the longing he felt in missing her would be his undoing. He'd have gotten right back in his truck and driven back to Storm just to be with her again.

He'd been a shit. No doubt. But he was an even bigger shit for coming back here and thinking Annie would forgive him.

If she gave him nothing but ice daggers for the rest of his days, he surely deserved it. She hadn't stopped him from going to Nashville. She told him to go. But he'd known she didn't want him to. And he couldn't stay. Storm was a wonderful place. But not for someone like him. And for each moment that passed since he'd been home, Chase had wondered why he'd even bothered to come back.

He walked through the grocery store and tried his best not to search the aisles like a lovesick teenager. He'd made an ass of himself coming here. What the hell had he expected? He was an old man. He'd had everything to offer Anna Mae all those years ago and now…now he couldn't even button his shirt without his hands shaking so badly he needed to take a pill to calm them. And even then, sometimes that wasn't enough.

He'd lived a long and full life that was full of booze, music, and women. He'd made a decision and he hadn't looked back. He deserved to die alone if that's what it came to.

The trembling in his hand started again, and Chase hurried to his truck, feeling the heat more than he normally did. He stumbled a few yards from his destination, but he didn't fall. Still, being unsteady on his feet was something he was never going to get used to and something he hoped he could ward off as long as possible.

He needed his music now more than ever.

Yanking on the truck door, he paused before climbing into the driver's seat. He paused with the door open just for a few seconds before putting the key in the ignition and gunning the engine. Before long, driving would be off the table and he'd be at the mercy of having someone else get him around.

A ball of fire burned high in his stomach and made his chest hurt. It seemed he got that a lot these days whenever he contemplated the future that was laid out ahead of him.

After slamming the door shut, he turned on the radio and blasted the a/c to keep from sweating. Then he put the truck in reverse and pulled out of the parking space. If he had any smarts at all, he'd get on the freeway and just keep driving. Somewhere. Anywhere. He couldn't go back to Nashville. But Storm didn't want him here. So why stay?

Chapter Seven

The buzzer on the oven sounded, pulling Anna Mae away from the towels and sheets she'd been folding in the laundry room.

It had been a long time since she'd baked a homemade pie the way her grandmother had taught her to when she was a little girl. She'd wanted to bake a peach pie, but peaches were so overpriced at the market now that they were out of season. Still, she'd been feeling nostalgic and in need of comfort after running into Chase, so she pulled out her recipe book and made the apple pie that she used to make with her grandmother every fall.

The sound of the buzzer grew louder the closer she got to the kitchen. So did the smell of the pie. After grabbing the potholders, she opened the oven door and peered into the oven. The ribbons of the piecrust looked beautifully browned to perfection. She'd made two pies. One for Rita Mae, Mary Louise, and Anna Mae's dinner. The other she'd set out on the table for the guests.

She pulled the pies out of the oven and set them down on a cooling rack on the counter by the opened window. As she set the second pie down, she noticed a truck outside by the curb. She didn't recognize the truck, but she knew all too well the man sitting inside of it.

How long had that hardheaded Chase Johnson been sitting out there in the hot sun?

* * * *

It had been a long time since Travis had gone straight home after closing up the pharmacy. Kristin made a habit of dropping by, even for a few minutes. He found the one thing that brightened his day since losing Jacob was to see her smile. But today she'd had a late appointment out of town.

He draped his arm across the steering wheel as he pulled his car out of the small parking lot behind the pharmacy, stopping at the stop sign and looking at the corner where the flower shop was located. He gave Pushing Up Daisies a quick glance. The lights were still on, and he could see the orange and black decorations in the windows, signaling the coming of Halloween. But he didn't see Kristin's car parked where it normally was, so he assumed she still hadn't returned to Storm.

He sighed. One night of not seeing Kristin didn't change how either of them felt each other. He loved her like he'd never loved another human being, save his children. And she understood just how deep his love for them ran.

And Celeste? Well, he'd always have feelings for her in some form. But anything special they'd had was long gone. He'd married her and they'd had children together. He owed it to her to help her through her grief over Jacob. But it had never been as it was with Kristin and it would never be.

His cell phone rang through his car radio and flashed with Lacey's number. Lacey wasn't the strong one. Sara Jane would always land on her feet. She was practical and for the most part, predictable. But Lacey was different. She was Travis's baby. Pressing the button on the dash, he answered the call quickly. "Lacey? What's wrong?"

"Mom's not home."

He frowned. "Did she say where she was going?"

"No."

Lacey didn't elaborate and Travis had to fight the groan working its way up his throat.

"What aren't you telling me?"

"She was weird this afternoon again. Drinking and looking at pictures. She's always looking at those pictures. And…"

"And what?"

Lacey didn't answer.

"Lacey, tell me. What happened?"

"She's drunk, Daddy. I saw her in the dining room crying as she looked through the photo album. Then when I was upstairs, I heard her leave the house and then start the car. When I looked out the window, I saw her driving away. I…was afraid she'd get into an accident, so I followed her."

"But you were upstairs. How could you have caught up with her? You weren't speeding, were you?" He'd already lost one child. He couldn't bear to lose another.

"No! Where else would she go but to the cemetery? So I stopped at the cemetery and saw her car parked there. I went to Jacob's grave and she was…" He heard Lacey's heavy sigh and waited. "She was stretched out on the ground crying with her face against Jacob's headstone."

Travis pulled over to the side of the road to give Lacey his full attention. He silently let out a curse and hit the steering wheel to let out his growing frustration. Lacey didn't need this. She had her own feelings to deal with. Hadn't their family gone through enough with Ginny Moreno's lies? Since learning that Ginny wasn't actually carrying their grandchild, Celeste had fallen deeper into despair, sometimes forgetting that she had two other children who were still alive and dealing with their own grief.

He heard the worry in Lacey's voice. She'd been trying to put on a brave face despite everything that had gone on in Storm and with their family. But if things didn't get better, she'd break, just like Celeste.

"Sweetie, I will take care of it. Don't let this worry you at all," he said warmly as he tapped his fingers on the steering wheel and tried to figure out how to handle the situation without causing more anxiety.

"But how is she going to drive home?" Lacey's voice broke. "You didn't see how much she drank earlier."

"I'll worry about her car later. You or Sara Jane can drive over to the cemetery with me later once I get your mother settled. Don't worry. It's going to be okay, sweetie."

"Okay. Daddy?"

"Yes?"

"I love you."

His heart squeezed. Hearing those words made him feel like a superhero. Like he could do anything to fix the wrongs that had been put upon his family. But as much as Travis knew Lacey meant them, he also knew he couldn't fix what couldn't be fixed.

Travis couldn't protect Lacey from everything. He didn't have the power to bring his boy back from the dead. And he couldn't stop people from talking about Ginny Moreno and her claim that she was carrying Jacob's baby. Or Dakota Alvarez's announcement in front of the entire town that the child Ginny carried was not Jacob's. It was Sebastian Rush's. He could only take away this momentary worry that fell on Lacey's shoulders.

"I love you too. Don't you worry. I'll take care of everything. I'll see you at home."

Travis pressed the button on the dash to disconnect the call and paused. She was his wife. If what Lacey said was true, he couldn't leave her at the cemetery in the state she was in, broken and unable to move forward in the wake of her despair.

After glancing in the rearview mirror to check if the road was clear, he pressed his foot on the gas and swung the car around so he could head toward the cemetery to collect his wife.

A few minutes later, he turned into the cemetery driveway and slowly made his way down the lane toward the plot where his son was buried. Sure enough, Celeste's car was parked askew with the nose of the car on the grass and the tail end of it on the pavement. He pulled his car up behind hers and shifted into park before killing the engine and pocketing the key in his jacket pocket.

With a heavy sigh, he pushed the car door open and stepped out into the hot Texas air. It had only been about fifteen minutes since he'd left the pharmacy but already the setting sun had made the evening air cooler. He didn't come to the cemetery often, but he knew exactly how to find Jacob's plot. He walked a few yards and stepped around one of the cottonwood trees with a park bench beneath it that had been strategically planted in the cemetery to give people a place to shade themselves while visiting a loved one's grave.

What Lacey had described to him was bad. But Travis wasn't prepared for what he saw when he finally reached Jacob's grave.

Celeste was stretched out on the grass in front of the headstone. When he reached her, her eyes were closed and her mouth was parted. Grass clippings were stuck to her cheek, most likely pasted there by her tears.

"Celeste," he said quietly as he bent down. Grabbing her arm, he gave her a gentle push to rouse her.

She didn't move but he heard her snoring quietly so he knew she was breathing.

"It's time to go home, Celeste," he said a little louder as he snaked his arm under her body to get her to sit up.

She moaned a little and whimpered and then her head fell back.

"Come on, Celeste. The groundkeeper will be here soon to lock the gate. We need to go."

"I don't...I...my baby...how." None of what Celeste was fighting to say made sense, but Travis got the gist of it. It had been the same thing for months. *My baby. How did this happen? I don't know how to live with this.*

She was dead weight in his arms even though she wasn't a big woman. Travis fought to help her to her feet and then he fought again to drag her to his car. When he reached the car, he wrestled with holding Celeste steady while he opened the passenger door and then got her settled enough so he could buckle her in. Before he closed the door, he rummaged through the glove compartment for a pen and a piece of paper. He found a pen, but had to settle for an envelope that had the pharmacy logo on it. It was full of old receipts that he emptied into the glove compartment before carefully shutting the car door and walking to Celeste's car. He wrote a quick note to the groundskeeper with the lie that the car had broken down and they'd be back in the morning to remove it. Travis listed his telephone number in case the groundskeeper had any questions and then slipped the envelope under the windshield wiper blade.

It had been a long day, he thought as he walked back to the car with a heavier step than he had when he'd arrived. He needed a smile and a way to forget the nightmare his life had become. He needed Kristin. But right now he needed to get Celeste home and to bed and then make sure that Lacey was okay. He'd deal with his own needs later.

* * * *

Ginny waddled into Cuppa Joe and looked around. Mid-afternoon, her sister's bakery was quiet. She quickly spotted Max sitting at a table.

"I'm glad you came," Ginny said, easing herself into the chair opposite Max.

"Why wouldn't I?"

Ginny shrugged. "I don't know. It's been really...weird here ever since the Founders' Day fiasco. When I heard you were coming to Storm, I nearly wept with joy. I've missed you."

"Me, too."

"How is it staying with your grandmother?"

"Great-grandmother. It's good to see her. She's getting old though. I hadn't seen her in a long time so I didn't realize just how old she was getting."

Hedda Garten, Max's great-grandmother, was the owner of the florist shop in town. She knew just about everyone and everything that happened in Storm.

"She's the one who told you about what happened." Ginny said. A swell of embarrassment rose up inside her. Max had come to Storm after Ginny's world had fallen apart. But Ginny hadn't been the one to tell him about it.

"Word gets around. But only because my mother asked what was happening in Storm. My mother knew that we were friends."

"And you came running."

"What are friends for?"

"Speaking of friends," Ginny said, determined to change the subject, "where's your friend, Scott? Didn't he come to Storm with you?"

"He decided to stop by and see Brittany. We ran into Marylee and Brittany Rush at the flower shop when we arrived."

A dull ache worked its way from her stomach to her chest. Brittany Rush had been Ginny's best friend and she'd failed that friendship miserably. She didn't have the slightest idea how or if that relationship could ever be repaired. There was a time when Brittany would have been the first person, aside from Jacob, that Ginny would have run to with a problem. She couldn't exactly run to Brittany now without causing her more pain.

Max seemed to sense Ginny's mood. "You know, we could have gone someplace for more than a cup of coffee. Someplace nicer."

Ginny chuckled. "Are you saying my sister's place isn't nice?"

"You know what I mean. Someplace where we could have had a burger or something."

Ginny shrugged. "This is practically the only place in town where I'm welcome these days."

"Slight exaggeration, don't you think? Your sister's place isn't the only one in town. Not everyone knows about what happened between you and the senator, and I'm sure not everyone cares."

"You don't know Storm. People will look you straight in the face and smile and then as soon as you turn your back, they're talking about you. I should know. It seems I can't get away from it."

"People are going to forget."

"You sound like my sister."

"She's right."

"Maybe they do in Austin. But not in Storm."

Max frowned. "Come on, it can't be that bad."

"Maybe. Maybe I'm just sensitive. Or maybe my hormones are just running wild. These days I never know."

Marisol came in from the kitchen. "Hey, when did you get here?" she asked with a smile when she saw Ginny.

Marisol loved having her home again, although she wasn't so happy about the reason. She looked at Ginny and then Max. "When you said you were waiting for someone, I didn't realize you were waiting for my sister. Let me get you both something hot from the oven."

"Thanks, Marisol," Ginny said.

Marisol grabbed a mug from the shelf and turned around to

ask, "So who's your friend, Ginny?"

"I've talked about Max before," Ginny said. "You might have met him at Jacob's funeral. Jacob, Brittany, and I were friends with Max at college."

"Right." Marisol made a face that showed her embarrassment. "You were Jacob's roommate. Honestly, there were so many people at his funeral, I don't remember seeing you."

"That's okay," Max said.

"What can I get for you, Max?"

"A soda is fine."

"A muffin too? These are Ginny's favorite."

"Sure thing."

Ginny licked her lips. "I swear I've eaten about a hundred of these since I found out I was pregnant. I can never resist them."

Marisol's expression turned sympathetic. "You and Jacob were close?"

Max looked at Ginny and then at Marisol. "I met Jacob the first day on campus. And then he introduced me to Ginny and Brittany." He glanced over at Ginny. "We all thought it was a crazy coincidence that they came from the same town where my great-grandmother lived. I never came to Storm much when I was a kid but I do remember how much I liked it here. We were all pretty much inseparable. Became best friends. I planned on coming down here to visit over the summer. Then the accident happened."

"Then I'm sorry for your loss. So I guess you know that Ginny and Jacob were best friends for years."

"Yes, ma'am."

He looked at Ginny and gave her a bittersweet smile. "That's why I'm glad I can be here for Ginny."

Ginny glanced over at Marisol, who was considering what Max had said. Max was a good friend. And Ginny couldn't afford to take any friendships for granted. She'd lost so much due to her own immaturity and naiveté.

Her mind immediately went to Logan. She'd lost a man she'd come to love and thought she might have a future with. Just thinking about Logan made her heart twist with pain. She'd loved Jacob. But as a friend. Logan was different. They'd grown so close and shared so many emotions that Ginny still couldn't believe she'd managed to trash everything with her lies.

"Earth to Ginny," Max said, leaning across the table. She'd been so lost in her thoughts about Logan that she hadn't realized Marisol had put a cup of hot chocolate in front of her along with a blueberry and raspberry muffin, one of her favorites.

"Sorry. Thinking about Logan." Ginny sighed, wondering if she'd made a mistake telling Max everything. But she so needed a friend. She reached for the muffin and immediately pulled off the top, loving the part with all the sugar and cinnamon on it. She popped a piece of it in her mouth. Usually one of her sister's famous muffins was enough to ease at least some of the pain she was feeling. But this time, it just tasted like sugar. She swallowed hard and then put the rest of the muffin top on a napkin.

"I take it you haven't talked to him since everything happened?" Max asked.

Ginny shifted in her seat uncomfortably. These days she no longer needed to use an excuse when she showed discomfort because people just assumed it was because she'd become so fat and pregnant.

She leaned back and placed her hand over her stomach. "I've tried. He won't talk to me. And I don't really blame him. What I did was inexcusable. I don't think he's ever going to forgive me for not telling him the truth."

Max shook his head. "People aren't perfect, Ginny."

She chuckled wryly. "Yeah? I don't even come close. I messed up big time. And Dakota Alvarez was only too happy to tell the whole town about it. Although...I can't blame her. She was...used by Sebastian Rush just as much as I was. It's easy to look back and see how it happened. It humiliates me to even think about it."

With the mention of the senator's name, Max winced. "How *did* that even happen?"

She sighed. "I really don't want to revisit it. Do you mind?"

"We don't have to talk about it ever again."

"Thanks. Do you remember that time we were all supposed to go to that mixer at the frat house off campus?" Ginny chuckled as the memory came back to her. It was their first semester on campus. "Jacob had just started dating that crazy girl. Oh, what was her name?"

Max laughed. "How could you forget? Fifi. Jacob said her curly hair made him feel like he was dating a poodle."

Ginny chuckled. "He never told me that."

"Okay, maybe it was me who said it. But he never disagreed."

"That one didn't last long but I sure remember that night of the 'almost' mixer."

"And the flat tire in the car with no spare tire and no jack stand."

Ginny laughed louder. "In the middle of nowhere and Fifi not being able to get service on her cell phone and yelling at Jacob to push the car until she was able to get some bars on her phone so she could call AAA."

Tears filled Max's eyes as he laughed. "It's a real shocker they didn't last that long."

"Yeah, I was happy when she was no longer around." Ginny played with her muffin top. "Do you remember you and Jacob and me and Brittany watching *The Twilight Zone* every night sitting on that old, ugly sofa you brought to the dorms with you?"

"The one with the springs popping out under the cushions?"

"How could you forget? I kept having to shift positions to keep from getting poked by springs."

Max's lips tilted to one side. "I never minded. You sat closer to me."

Ginny took in his words and quickly dismissed them. Jacob had told her once that Max had confided in him that he thought of Ginny as more than a friend. But nothing had ever happened between them, and Ginny had never had those kinds of feelings for Max.

"That sofa was ridiculously ugly though, huh?"

"What did you do with it when you moved out of the dorms?"

"We had it in the apartment we rented, but then it got so bad we had to burn it. Me and a few of the guys cut it up in about a hundred pieces and had a big bonfire." Max reached across the table and picked up a piece of her muffin, then quickly ate it. He made a face that showed his approval. "These are good."

Ginny pulled her plate with the muffin toward her. "Eat your own. This one is mine. You had a bonfire? You could have gotten arrested for that."

"Almost did. Someone called the fire department and when they showed up, we told the fire chief that we'd been studying late for finals and one of the desk lamps fell into the sofa cushion. It caught on fire so we had to take the sofa out to the backyard to save it from burning down the house."

Ginny laughed. "And he believed you?"

"I don't know. He seemed impressed. I just think our story was so brilliant that he gave us a pass." Max smiled and took a sip of his drink. "Those were the good old days."

A feeling of sadness enveloped Ginny as she felt the baby move inside her. Little Bit could be Jacob's baby. She so wanted it to be. Maybe. But she wouldn't know for a while.

Max reached across the table for her hand.

Leaning forward, she gave his hand a squeeze in thanks.

"What is it?"

"I just really miss Jacob. I wonder sometimes what he'd be saying to me now after everything that's gone on."

"He'd be there for you no matter what. I'm just really glad you called me. I'm glad I can be here for you."

The bell over the door rang. Both Ginny and Max turned to see who was coming through. As soon as Ginny saw Logan's face, she snatched her hand away.

"Logan!"

His eyes were like ice as he glared at her from the doorway. It was all deserved. He'd opened himself to her completely about his struggles and she hadn't done the same. She'd held back. She could argue that she truly believed that the baby she was carrying was Jacob Salt's. She had no idea that Jacob was infertile.

But that was beside the point. She hadn't been honest. She realized now that it wouldn't have been easy for Logan to hear about her affair with Sebastian Rush. Things may not have moved in the direction they had between them. But she should have at least given Logan the chance to hear the truth and come to terms with it. Her omission was a lie even if she hadn't uttered the words.

His eyes remained fixed on her for a moment and then turned to Max.

She stood up from the table. "Logan, have you met Max?"

"I'm not here to see you, Ginny," he said flatly. "Or your friend."

Her breath caught in her throat as she stifled a sob. When was it going to get easier to see Logan? Would there ever be a time when he wouldn't hate her as he did now?

Logan walked to the counter where Marisol was busy putting out pastries she'd just taken out of the oven.

"Hi, Marisol," Logan said. "My mother sent me over to pick up something special you were making for her?"

"It's in the refrigerator out back. Someone having a birthday tonight?"

"Just a customer from out of town. I don't know who it is. She wants to have a little family party at the pub tonight and you know my mother. She volunteered to organize it."

"Well, that was nice of her. Give me a second and I'll be right back with the cake," Marisol said, pasting on a smile for Logan. As Marisol slipped into the back room, Ginny could see her sister struggling to remain professional even though she knew Logan's brush-off was killing Ginny.

Ginny had done this. She'd been the one to create this. She'd brought this on the family and now her sister's business could suffer because of it. Sure, Sonya Murphy wouldn't hold it against Marisol that Ginny had lied to her son. But Sonya Murphy couldn't buy enough cakes and pastries to keep Cuppa Joe afloat.

The tension in the room was palpable and more than Ginny could stand.

Look at me, Logan. But he wouldn't.

When it became too much for Ginny, she blurted out, "I'll see you at home, Marisol." Logan didn't turn to look at Ginny or Max when they both stood up to leave. "I'll see you, too, Logan?"

He didn't answer. It was as if she wasn't even there. And maybe that's what it had come to.

"Come on, Ginny," Max said, holding the door open for her.

She looked back once, just to see if he would turn to look at her. Then she let Max lead her out the door and walk her down the street to her car. She'd wait to cry, because she knew the tears would come again. She just wouldn't do it in the middle of Storm where people could see her. She wasn't about to give them more talk. She'd already given them enough to last a lifetime.

Chapter Eight

Logan felt the rush of hot air against his back and willed himself to keep from turning around. Who the fuck was this guy with Ginny? Had she already found someone else to lie to?

Marisol came in from the back room with a sheet cake in her hand. "What do you think?" she asked, showing him the cake.

He didn't care about the damned cake. He wished he hadn't even come here to pick it up. "It's fine."

"Fine? Since when has one of my cakes been just fine?"

Logan shrugged and pulled his wallet out of his back pocket. "How much do I owe you?"

"I'll just put it on your mother's account."

"Fine."

He watched as Marisol carefully placed the cake into a box.

"It's good to see you, Logan," Marisol said, closing the box. She reached for the tape dispenser on the counter, cut a small piece, and secured the box.

Then she pushed it closer to the end of the counter.

He should say something. But Logan didn't really know what to say to Marisol. She was Ginny's sister.

"I've been busy."

"That's bullshit and you know it. You're avoiding Ginny because you're hurt."

He drew in a deep breath and reached for the box, but Marisol put her hand on his, stopping him.

"She's hurting, too, Logan," she said. "I know you don't believe that because you think she somehow did this on purpose. But she didn't. I know she loved you. She still loves you."

"Really? It didn't look that way to me," Logan said.

Marisol frowned. "You mean Max?"

"I don't care who the guy is. I don't want to know anything about it."

"He was Jacob's roommate and Ginny's friend from college. As far as I know, that's all they are."

She let go of the box and Logan quickly retrieved it from the counter. "Well, we don't always know everything. Do we?"

His heart pumping, Logan pushed through the door to the sidewalk and started walking back to Murphy's. Ginny was a damned liar. There was no way to move on from that. But no matter what Marisol said, it looked like she already had.

Logan just wished it didn't feel like a kick in the gut.

* * * *

Anna Mae glanced out the window once again at that fool of a man who still sat in the truck. He had the windows down, which meant that he wasn't running the a/c, but it was unseasonably hot today, and she knew he had to be melting in the cab, especially since he was used to Nashville weather, and it tended to be at least ten degrees cooler than central Texas this time of the year.

Still, his comfort was hardly her problem. She'd kicked the habit of worrying about Chase Johnson years ago and she wasn't about to start up that addiction again.

She grabbed a rag and started wiping down the counters.

Then again, it would be terribly inconvenient if he got heat stroke. After all, if she let the man die right there in front of the house, that would be terrible for the business she and her sister worked so hard to build.

Telling herself she was only watching out for the B&B, she grabbed a bottle of cold water from the refrigerator and then headed out the kitchen door. The chrysanthemums she'd planted last week in the side garden patio had taken root and were starting to grow. But she couldn't appreciate the fruits of her labor until she got rid of Chase.

As she approached the truck, she saw that now the driver's side door was open and one of his boots was on the pavement. The closer she got to the truck, the more he came into view. The passenger side window was open and he was fiddling with something in the front seat of his car.

Well, at least she wouldn't find him dead. The sooner Anna Mae could get him to close the truck door and drive away, the better she'd feel.

"What the devil are you doing outside my house?" she said when she finally reached the truck. She peered in the passenger's side window and immediately was taken aback by what she saw. It was a little kitten, probably no more than a couple of months old. Her heart melted.

"Yours?" he asked.

"What? No. We don't have any cats here. Where did you find him… her… whatever?"

He picked up the kitten and pressed his lips to its nose. Then he inspected its parts before placing it back in the cowboy hat. "I think it's a her. But I'm not sure. I found her running back and forth in the road a little ways down the street. If I'd been driving any faster I would have hit her."

"What was she doing in the road?"

"Chasing a field mouse that was intent on not being caught. She wasn't paying attention."

Anna Mae's irritation gone, she opened the passenger side door and inspected the little kitten who was curled up inside Chase's cowboy hat.

"Is that bottle of water for me?" Chase asked.

"Uh, yeah, I brought it out for you. I thought maybe you were… Oh, it doesn't matter. Here." She handed him the bottle of water, which he opened right away. But instead of taking a sip of the water himself, Chase poured a few tablespoons in the palm of his wide hand and offered it to the kitten. The kitten stood up inside the overturned hat and went straight for the water, lapping at the liquid until it was gone.

"What are you going to do with her?" Anna Mae asked.

"I don't know. Why don't you take her?"

"Me? I can't have a cat here. Some of our guests are allergic to cats. Beside, Rita Mae will have a fit if she starts scratching the furniture."

Chase poured a little more water in his hand and offered it to the kitten. "Well, I guess I'm just going to have to take you home with me, little one."

Feeling the sun beating down on her head, Anna Mae said, "You? What do you know about taking care of another living creature?"

He glanced up at her and smiled. "I grew up on a ranch, didn't I?"

She shrugged, feeling slightly foolish for her quick judgment. "It's been years since you worked on a ranch, Chase. Did you have a dog or cat when you were in Nashville?"

He shook his head. "I couldn't. The hours I kept were too crazy to know when I'd be home to take care of a pet. Maybe my brother's grandkids will have fun playing with her out in the barn. I'm sure they'd like that."

Chase picked up the kitten again. She looked impossibly lost in his hands. She was so tiny. So vulnerable. And he held her so gently.

Oh, Lordy, Anna Mae, he was just holding a cat.

"What are you doing here?" she asked.

He put the kitten on his shoulder. "I should think it's obvious. I came to see you."

"Again? Why do you keep doing this, Chase? I don't know how to make myself more clear than I've been. What we had was over a long time ago and there is nothing left for us to say to each other. We've lived a lifetime without each other. I don't want to see you."

His smile was slow in coming, but when it finally took hold, it spread wide across his face. "If you don't want to see me, why did you come out here?"

She opened her mouth to argue, but then closed it quickly. She didn't have an answer to that. Well, not a good enough answer.

The truth was, ever since Chase had come back to Storm, it wasn't that Anna Mae didn't want to see him. She feared seeing him.

Over the years it had been easy to blame Chase for his leaving even though she'd given him her blessing to go. But deep down, she hadn't believed he'd stay away. And then when he was gone and she found out she was carrying his child, it made it all the harder to call him and ask him to come home.

The anger that had built up over the years, that had replaced the heartache of losing Chase and their child, had kept her going. She knew that now. It was a bitter pill to swallow. But now that Chase was standing just feet away from her, she couldn't ignore it. She'd never stopped loving him. All those feelings she'd felt as a young woman were still alive inside her. If she didn't deal with it now, it would only crush her again when Chase left Storm.

The kitten was still climbing around Chase's shoulders. Seeing the strong, sexy man and the adorable kitten made it hard for her to hang on to any of the anger that still lingered.

"The water was for you. I thought you were going to shrivel up and die in this heat. You know, this isn't Nashville. It's still as hot as hell down here. People die of heat stroke."

"I thank you for the water and so does Patsy."

"Patsy? You mean you've already named her?"

"Sure. Why not?"

He picked up the kitten and gazed at her face. The light in his blue eyes burned as bright as it did when they'd been lovers. There was a time Chase held her as lovingly and gently as he was holding that kitten. It was more than Anna Mae could take.

"She's going to pee on you."

The sound of his chuckle was low and rough. "I've had worse."

"Gross."

"I meant that metaphorically."

"Oh. Well, I'll leave you to her."

Anna Mae started up the walkway toward the house. She did what she'd come out there to do. She'd given Chase Johnson a bottle of cold water and made sure he wasn't dead. She didn't have any more time to waste on nostalgia.

"Anna Mae?"

Don't turn around again!

"What now?"

"Do you have a box?"

She turned to look at Chase then and saw that Patsy was climbing up his arm. Sighing, she waved for him to come into the house.

A few minutes later they were in the utility room going through different sized boxes that were left over from deliveries that had recently been made to the bed and breakfast. Chase wrestled with the kitten, who was a bundle of energy now that she was hydrated and out of the heat.

"This one is a good size. It'll fit in the passenger's seat so you can drive home." Anna Mae brought the box out into the kitchen and put it on the floor. "Why don't you let her try it?"

Chase gently placed the kitten in the box. She was none too happy with suddenly being confined and started to meow.

"Maybe she's hungry," Anna Mae said, going to the cabinet and then rummaging through it to see what she had. "We've never had a cat so I don't have anything to give her."

"Do you have a can of tuna?"

"Ah, of course. I just happen to have a few."

She pulled out two cans of tuna from the cabinet, opened one of them with a can opener, and scooped a small portion into a small red plastic bowl that had been drying in the sink. She handed the bowl to Chase, who gave it to the kitten. Then she grabbed another red bowl and and filled it with water.

Patsy tackled the tuna first, going to town as if she hadn't eaten in days.

Anna Mae reached in and ran her fingers over the kitten's soft fur as she ate. The kitten's purring sounded like a motor reverberating inside the box.

"It's a good thing you found her," she said.

"I guess Patsy and I found each other."

Anna Mae stood up straight and looked at Chase. In all the years she'd convinced herself that she hated him, she never imagined this sweet and vulnerable side of him. She'd convinced herself Chase had been selfish and unfeeling. She'd even convinced herself that he'd never loved her. Certainly not as much as she'd loved him.

But looking at him now, she wondered if she'd sold Chase short. She wasn't a perfect woman by any stretch of the imagination. But perhaps Chase wasn't deserving of the hate she'd laid on him all these years.

When she'd been standing at the truck, she told herself she wouldn't ask him. But curiosity was getting the better of her. "You were awfully quick to name her. Where does Patsy come from?"

"You're kidding, right?"

She shook her head.

"Patsy Cline?"

Anna Mae frowned. "You...you named the kitten after Patsy Cline?"

He nodded. "Don't you remember that night down at the lake?"

"Which one?"

"The night after that gig with your brother George over in San Antonio. We drove all the way home with the instruments and the PA system bouncing in the back of truck and decided to ditch George and your sister-in-law because they'd been fighting the entire night."

There'd been so many memories, but this one tumbled back as if it were yesterday.

Anna Mae smiled. "She kept complaining they didn't have room for all the equipment in that stupid VW Bug she'd bought that day. I never thought that thing would make the trip to begin with but she insisted on bringing it despite my brother wanting to take his own truck. That was long before Mary Louise was born."

"We were following them to make sure the car wouldn't break down. But we pulled off the highway and lost them just before we got to Storm."

"We decided to camp out by the lake," she said as the memories flashed before her eyes. "Except we had no tent."

"We were being spontaneous."

"We were being stupid. We had no blanket."

"We had each other, Annie." Chase pulled her into his arms and to her surprise, Anna Mae let him. He rested his cheek against hers and started to hum as his feet moved to and fro.

"Dance with me," he whispered.

Her head was swimming. "There's no music."

"I can fix that." And he began to sing. "*Crazy. I'm crazy for feeling so lonely.*"

A lump formed in her throat. "How could I forget that?"

"*I'm crazy…*"

He continued to sing softly against her ear. She danced with him slowly as she listened to him, and suddenly she was there at the lake again. The truck radio was playing the Patsy Cline ballad and they danced under the light of a near full moon. And then because the bugs were too plentiful and the instruments were in the bed of the truck, she and Chase locked themselves inside the cab and they made love for the first time.

"You feel good in my arms, Anna Mae Prager," Chase whispered. "But then, you always did."

Her heart swelled with emotion she didn't want to feel. And yet she was there in Chase's arms, a mature woman in the twilight of her life having lived without the man who had been the love of her life. What would their life have been like had they shared moments like this all these years? Her heart broke for what wasn't, but at the same time, she didn't want to let go of Chase.

Chase stopped dancing and tilted her chin with his fingers so she was forced to look at him.

"I hope that wherever you end up going…whenever you end up leaving here, you'll be able to keep Patsy," Anna Mae said.

"I'm not going anywhere, Annie. And I'm not letting go of you again." Chase lowered his head and covered her mouth with his. It shocked her at first, but she was powerless to stop it. Her entire body exploded with emotion and a desire she thought was dormant in her. Nonexistent even. She'd thought she'd lived a full life, but it had been a lie. A bigger lie than she'd ever told herself. She now knew she'd been dead inside all these years, pushing away feelings that had become too painful for her to bear without Chase.

He slipped his arm around her waist and pulled her closer to him. He kissed her cheek and then made a trail of kisses along her neck until she moaned softly.

The realization that came over Anna Mae leveled her. She'd been a shell all these years. And now with one kiss, Chase had managed to fill her again.

Patsy began to meow, pulling Anna Mae from being lost in Chase's touch. She heard the front door slam and realized they were no longer alone.

"Anna Mae?"

She took a step out of Chase's arms when she heard Rita Mae's voice. When she peered up into his face, she saw red-hot desire. His blue eyes had turned a smoky gray and his skin was flushed.

"Whose truck is out front?"

Rita Mae walked into the kitchen and stopped short. "What the hell is going on in here?"

Chapter Nine

It was hot as hell in Sebastian Rush's office even with the air conditioning on full blast. The journalists who had come out to interview him about a proposed veteran's center had brought hot lights and equipment that was sucking up the oxygen in the room. But having an interview out in the square where disaster had struck at the hands of Dakota Alvarez was bad karma.

Sebastian pulled at the collar of the crisp white shirt his mother had insisted he change into when the crew had arrived. She was right of course, but at his age he didn't really need Marylee Rush henpecking him about such details.

He frowned, realizing that he was being defensive, but he was in a pissy mood. He'd made the call to Logan Murphy as promised and asked him to appear in the newscast with him. The military was a brotherhood, and he'd counted on Logan to feel that camaraderie and support the proposed center in Storm. With Logan on board, Sebastian would be able to change the dialogue from the disastrous Founders' Day fiasco to something that would pull at the heartstrings of patriotic Texans whose support he'd need on Election Day.

But Logan had turned him down flat. He didn't want to hear

anything Sebastian had to say. When his mother found out, she'd called the reporter anyway saying they could still move forward with using Logan Murphy as a mascot for this project even if he wasn't a willing participant. As for the veterans' center, it would get bogged down in committee and red tape and probably redlined out of the budget before it ever became a reality. But that didn't mean he couldn't use Logan Murphy and his war hero status to help him appeal to voters during the election. Once he held office, he could explain away why a veterans' center near Storm wouldn't work, and Sebastian could move on to other things.

"It'll only be a few more minutes before we can get started."

"Good," Marylee said. "It's important the voters know about the senator's accomplishments and that he has a solid plan for improving the lives of veterans returning from military service. This will be on the air tonight, won't it?"

The reporter glanced at her notebook. "Well, that's up to my producer. He may want to run the segment tomorrow."

"During prime time?" Marylee pressed.

The girl smiled. "Possibly." She pulled at her blue blouse and blew out a quick breath. "Maybe we should have the interview outside. It's very hot in here and the light is not as good."

"I think it's best we focus on the campaign office," Marylee said.

"Well, we could have the interview out in front on the sidewalk. My crew could get some pictures of the square and of course, the headquarters sign. I think it shows you're more in touch with the community when you're among the citizens of Storm."

The girl was playing with him. She didn't give a good goddamn where the interview was held as long as she didn't look like a sweaty mess doing it. She was a pretty young thing in her mid-twenties. Probably doing her best to make a name for herself and move up the ranks to anchor and then eventually a network position. When Marylee had called to set up the meeting, the girl had pounced on the chance to come to Storm and interview a senator who was up for reelection. His mother had made it clear that the interview was to focus on his plans to help veterans, and in particular, to celebrate the return of Logan Murphy, Storm's very own war hero.

People would eat this up. The news would surely switch focus from the story of Sebastian's philandering ways with young women to something more relevant in voters' minds.

"Of course," he said amiably. "I think moving the interview outside is a wonderful idea."

* * * *

"Marisol sure does bake a beautiful cake," Sonya said, looking at the cake that Logan had just brought back to the pub. She closed the cake box after quickly inspecting it. "I'd better get this in the refrigerator or all the frosting will melt before the birthday girl arrives. Are you going to be working a shift tonight, son?"

Logan lifted the hinged section of the bar top that separated the space behind the bar from the rest of the pub. "Why? How big is this birthday party going to be?"

"Oh, it's just a family from out of town. But since they're on the road, they wanted to make it special for their little girl who is missing a birthday party at home. But I saw some news crews in town earlier when I was shopping and I wondered what that was all about. I thought maybe they were having a concert in the square."

Logan cringed. "*Damned press.*"

Sonya looked at Logan with a sympathetic motherly eye. "Well, despite Storm's insignificance to the entire state of Texas, we do have a state senator who lives here, who's running for reelection, and who's news-worthy. Or at least gossip-worthy," she amended with a frown.

Logan blew out a breath. "Rush is trying to spin this whole Dakota and Ginny bullshit to his advantage."

"Watch your mouth," Sonya said, giving him a quick warning glance.

"Sorry."

Sonya picked up the cake box. "What makes you think that?"

"He called me."

"What? Sebastian Rush had the gall to call you again?" Sonya took a protective step toward him. "What did he want with you?"

"It's okay, Mom. It's the same old thing. He wanted to parade me out to the press as if he had anything to do with my service in the military. As if that makes him something special."

"What an ass!"

Logan chuckled at the apologetic look Sonya cast him.

"Don't worry. I told Rush to get lost. I'm not going to be his little puppet."

"Thank God. He dug his own grave. Now let him lie in it."

His mother disappeared into the kitchen and left him behind the bar. It was early, but already the place was hopping which was just as well, since a slow bar meant too much time to think about Ginny or Sebastian Rush or anything else. Better to just lose himself in his work.

Tate Johnson and Mary Louise Prager sat at the end of the bar and talked. Every once in a while he'd walk down to where they were sitting to see if they wanted another drink or some food.

Logan had left it to his mother to handle the birthday party for the family who was just passing through town, although Logan did lend his voice to sing Happy Birthday, which made the little girl who was turning ten years old while on vacation very happy.

Logan was putting dirty glasses into a rack at the bar when his brother Patrick came into Murphy's. He waved as Patrick made his way to the bar. He was still dressed in his EMT uniform instead of his normal jeans and T-shirt.

"Just getting off a shift?" Logan asked.

Patrick shook his head. "I just dropped off a patient at the hospital and saw the news crew setting up in front of Rush's headquarters. Did you know Sebastian was giving an interview today?"

"I don't care what that piece of shit is doing. Want a beer?"

Patrick slid onto the barstool and shook his head. "I'm still on duty."

"Then what are you doing here?"

"Anyone around who can relieve you behind the bar for a few?" Patrick asked.

Logan didn't like the sound of Patrick's voice. "Mom's in the back doing the books. Why?"

"Get her to come out here. You're going to want to see this."

"See what? What the hell are you talking about?"

"Senator Rush is giving an interview and you're the star topic."

Logan slammed a fist on the bar top. "That no good sonuvabitch!"

* * * *

"I don't want to hear it." Anna Mae said. There'd never been a time she couldn't look her sister in the eye, but today was a first. It was a first for a lot of things.

Anna Mae could still feel Chase's lips on her mouth. His kiss was more than what she'd remembered all these years. When she'd allowed herself to remember at all. But right now she was facing her sister's wrath. Well, maybe that was overstating it a bit. Although when Rita Mae had practically run Chase out to his car she hadn't exactly been full of sunshine and happiness.

"Well, you're going to. You were practically making out—"

"Making out? For God's sake, we aren't teenagers."

"Could have fooled me."

Anna Mae fisted her hands in frustration. "I thought you were the one who said I needed to talk to Chase about what happened. That I couldn't ignore it. Well, we talked."

Rita Mae folded her hands across her chest. "Is that what that was?"

"What did you think was going to happen?"

Rita Mae's arms fell to her side. "I don't know. It's always bothered me that you've spent your life alone. Ever since the baby—"

"Don't!" Anna Mae warned.

"You've shut yourself off from having any kind of a life without Chase. Don't get me wrong. I get it. George and Chase are cut from the same cloth. Men like that are better left for women with shallow expectations. But that's not you, Anna Mae. You don't want that kind of life."

"How would you know that?"

Rita Mae took a step back. "Because I know you better than anyone else in the world."

"Really?"

"Yes, really."

The years tumbled in front of her. It was easy to be comfortable in the life she'd led since Chase had left Storm. But now that Chase was back, that little piece of her, the one that she'd buried along with the child they'd lost, was screaming out to her to remember who she was. She couldn't go back. That would never work. But she had been dead inside. She hadn't even tried to make a life and ended up a spinster. Sure, she had a couple of nice businesses with her sister. But that's all she'd allowed herself over the years. She'd never taken the chance for something more that might have led her out of Storm.

She looked at Rita Mae and the realization that life had moved on without her was glaringly obvious. The reason why she'd come home from New York City after that brief time of living there, the reason she'd stayed in Storm when she knew Chase was leaving, was no longer valid.

"I know it's been a long time, Rita Mae. But surely you remember what it was like to be in love."

Sadness flashed across Rita Mae's face. "This isn't about me. Vietnam killed a lot of dreams for a lot of people. Not just mine. Unlike you, the man I loved died. He's never coming back."

"I know. And I'm not trying to minimize that. But the reasons I came back to Storm are no longer valid. Our parents died a long time ago. We built a life here and practically raised Mary Louise by ourselves. And she's a fine woman who doesn't need us the way she did."

"What are you saying?"

She braced herself, not sure how Rita Mae would take what she was about to say. "I realized something today. I never stopped loving Chase Johnson."

"Did you tell him that?"

"No." She placed her hands on her face, feeling the rush of blood that her admission had given her.

"Well, that's good. He's liable to take advantage of that, and you, if you tell him."

"I'm not a child. I'm an old woman."

Rita Mae *pffted* and looked away.

"Well, I am," Anna Mae insisted. "I have fewer days ahead of me than I have behind me and I don't want to waste the days I have left wrestling with regrets. I've had too many years of that."

"Anna Mae, listen to yourself. You have no reason to believe he'll stay here in Storm. His life is in Nashville. With music. Your life is here. So what do you do if he decides to go back again? I don't want to see you go through that heartache all over again."

"It might be different. I don't know."

"Where do you think our brother is right now?"

She shrugged.

"Yeah, there you go. Neither do I. We get a Christmas card and a birthday card for Mary Louise and that's pretty much it."

"George isn't that bad."

"Who are you kidding? He's practically a stranger to his daughter and Chase hasn't been much better. Don't start something that is only going to end with you watching Chase Johnson's taillights heading out of Storm. I won't hear of it."

"What's wrong with finding out if there is still something there? Maybe capturing a piece of happiness that was missing?"

Rita Mae paced in front of her. "Have you been hearing me?"

"Yes. You're afraid Chase is going to leave again. Well…maybe he will. But isn't that my decision to make? Can't I at least have this time in my life without worrying about how it will affect anyone else?"

The shocked look on Rita Mae's face made Anna Mae want to snatch her words back.

"You'd leave Storm? After all these years?"

Anna Mae sighed. "I don't know."

Her sister collapsed into a chair at the table. "Yes, you do. You're actually considering making the same mistake again."

"It wasn't a mistake for me to stay in Storm, Rita Mae. You needed me. You're my sister and I was glad to be here for you. And you were there for me during the most difficult time in my life."

"But you resent me for it."

Anna Mae shook her head.

"Anna Mae, I never wanted you to give up your life for me. If I had known that was how you felt, I…"

The look of regret on her sister's face was not what Anna Mae had wanted at all.

"Life's too short," Rita Mae said. "We both know that. I did need you back then. But I never wanted to hold you back from happiness. I thought you wanted to stay in Storm."

"I did. I do. And if Chase Johnson leaves Storm again, then who knows what will happen? But I do know that he's the only man I've ever loved. Neither one of us is getting any younger. If I don't at least try to find out if there is something worth having together, I know I will regret it."

Tears filled her sister's eyes. "I hope you know what you're doing."

Chapter Ten

Ginny stood outside of Cuppa Joe, waiting for Marisol to close the shop. Luis was out tonight with Mallory, which meant that no one had to rush home and make dinner. Marisol had insisted that the best way to stop talk was to be seen out in public as if nothing had happened.

She didn't believe her sister, but Ginny wasn't about to hide any longer. Marisol locked the door to Cuppa Joe and met Ginny on the sidewalk.

"Are you ready to go?" she asked.

"Where are we going?"

"Pizza. We haven't had a good pizza in a long time."

Ginny's mouth immediately started to water. "Did you want to get the car and drive to a pizza place?"

Marisol frowned. "What for? The best pizza in town is right around the corner."

"You mean the one across the street from Sebastian Rush's campaign headquarters?"

Marisol waved her off. "It's late. Everyone has probably gone home by now. You don't have to worry about it."

They walked down Cedar Street and turned left onto 2nd Street. As soon as they turned the corner they saw a big ruckus in front of Rush's campaign office.

"What the hell is going on?" Marisol asked.

"I have no idea."

There was a small crowd of people surrounding the news crew that was set up on the sidewalk with cameras and bright lights. Ginny immediately spotted Patrick Murphy who was dressed in his uniform.

"Patrick's here," Marisol said.

"I hope no one was hurt." Ginny spotted Logan standing in front of Sebastian Rush. "What is Logan doing here?"

Ginny followed Marisol down the street toward the crowd as quickly as she could in her condition. She didn't want to get too close, so she grabbed Marisol by the arm and stood across the street in front of the hair salon so people wouldn't notice them.

"I told you I didn't want anything to do with this, Rush. But you just don't get it. You can't force your way into everyone's life. I want no part of you!"

Ginny could hear Logan's voice booming above the chatter of the crowd. The news crew's camera was trained on him as he screamed at Sebastian. Patrick was now right behind Logan, holding him back from getting close enough to strike Sebastian. Oh, but Ginny wished he could. She had never seen Logan this angry before, even when he'd found out about the affair. He'd been more hurt with her than angry.

Of course the senator could drive anyone to distraction. And Lord knew that Logan had reason enough to be furious with him.

"I want you to leave me alone! I want no part of you or your fucking campaign. As far as I'm concerned, you can rot in hell. Haven't you done enough to destroy the good people of Storm?"

Patrick pulled Logan back, but the cameraman followed. A young woman with a microphone rushed to catch up to Patrick and Logan, who were now walking down 2nd Street. She stuck the microphone in Logan's face and asked a question that Ginny couldn't hear, but Logan pushed the microphone away and kept walking.

"You're going to pay for this, Murphy," Sebastian called out. "You and your girlfriend will pay for blackening my name!"

Logan stopped and turned around. "You did that one all by yourself, Rush. Don't you forget it."

As the cameraman and the female reporter ran back to the

campaign headquarters, Logan turned and saw Ginny standing across the street. Her heart pounded in her chest.

"Give me a minute, Marisol," Ginny said. She walked across the street and met Logan at the corner by the bank where no one on 2nd Street could see them. Patrick and Marisol stood on the corner on the other side of the building, most likely to give them a few moments of privacy.

"What do you want?" Logan asked. She could tell by the way he paced that he was still shaking with anger.

"Nothing," she said. "I just want to say that...you did the right thing."

"What did I do? I told off Sebastian Rush. Big deal. The guy's a prick."

A weak smile pulled at Ginny's face. "It's a very big deal, Logan. You know that men like Sebastian Rush think they can get away with everything. They don't care who they hurt as long as they get what they want. He wanted to use you and you wouldn't let him. I wish I'd been as strong as you."

"I only made things worse. If Twitter and Facebook haven't seen enough action on the scandals of Storm, they're about to."

"So what?"

Logan's eyes widened. "So what? You don't care that people are going to be talking about you and your baby?"

"Sure, I care. But I care more that you stood up for what's right. That makes it worth it."

He stared at her for a long moment. Ginny would give anything to know what was going through his mind. She'd destroyed the most wonderful relationship she'd ever shared. She loved Logan.

"It's not hard to stand up and do the right thing, Ginny. Sometimes that's all there is."

He turned away from her and headed down Cedar Street toward Murphy's Pub. She waited until he'd reached the corner by Cuppa Joe to turn around and find Marisol.

Patrick glanced at Ginny as she approached. "I'd better make sure he's okay," he said. "Goodnight, Marisol."

"Bye."

Ginny stood there and looked at the chaos happening at the end of the street. The crowd was still gathered outside of Sebastian's office, but Sebastian had disappeared along with Marylee.

She looked at her sister. "I'm not so hungry, Marisol. Do you mind if we skip pizza tonight?"

Marisol's gaze followed Patrick. "I've lost my appetite, too."

* * * *

When he was young, Chase had loved to sit on the back porch and listen to the sounds of the animals in the barn. The night had cooled the air off considerably. Patsy sat on his lap and tried to climb his chest, digging her tiny claws into his shirt to give her leverage.

As he had suspected, Zeke wasn't too happy about Chase bringing a kitten home to the ranch, especially when Chase suggested Carol and Danny would love to play with her. He wasn't going to be able to care for Patsy forever. Maybe it was unfair of him to burden his brother yet again with a responsibility that should have been his.

The screen door slapped against the wooden frame causing Chase to turn. Zeke walked over slowly, his boots hitting the floorboards with purpose.

Chase's shoulders sagged. He didn't have the energy to go at it with his brother. But instead of Zeke giving him a hard time, he eased down in the chair next to Chase and sighed.

"What's going on, Chase?"

"How do you mean?"

"You never asked me if I wanted to stay," Zeke said. "Never once. You had your dreams and it didn't matter what it cost everyone else for you to have them."

The kitten climbed up his shirt and meowed.

"It's been forty years, Chase. I really hated you for leaving here and leaving me with the running of the ranch."

"You love this ranch."

"Now. I didn't then. I didn't want to take over for Daddy any more than you did. I didn't know what I wanted back then. Not like you. It wasn't until I met Alice that the pieces of the man I could be fell into place. But I always hated you for forcing this on me."

It was a hard thing for Chase to hear, but it was a long time coming.

"How long?" Zeke asked.

Chase thought about the secret he carried with him. He wasn't going to be able to carry it alone forever. If not Zeke, who could he trust?

Zeke's voice grew louder, more urgent. "Dammit, how long are you going to be here? I have to know."

"I'm sick, Zeke."

Zeke frowned. "Sick?"

"Parkinson's. I got the diagnosis from a doc in Nashville."

Zeke closed his eyes and pinched the bridge of his nose. When he lifted his head again, he asked. "How long have you known?"

"A while. The symptoms didn't show up right away. But they're getting worse. Right now they're manageable."

"I noticed you shaking some. I didn't think it was anything more than age."

"Good. I prefer this not get around until I have no choice. I just want to live. I need you, Zeke. I don't know what's coming down the road but I do know I need you. I want to live out the rest of my life here on the ranch as long as you're okay with it."

Zeke looked at him for a long time. "This has always been your home. Where else would you go if not here?"

"Thank you."

Zeke got up from the chair and placed his hand on Chase's shoulder. "I love you, brother. Despite everything, I always have."

"Me, too."

Headlights shown in the driveway by the gate. Chase looked that way but couldn't make out the car.

"That doesn't look like one of the boys' trucks. Are you expecting company?" Chase asked.

"No. That looks like Anna Mae's car."

His heart pounded in his chest. Ever since he'd danced with Anna Mae in the kitchen and held her in his arms, he could think of nothing else.

"Does she know?" Zeke asked.

Chase shook his head. "I don't know how to tell her something like this."

Zeke dragged in a deep breath. "She'll find out soon enough, I suppose. I'll let you have your moment with her."

By the time Zeke walked into the house, Anna Mae had parked her car and was already getting out. She stood by the car and looked at Chase as if she were unsure. With so little light, it was hard to tell that they were both forty years older than the last time they'd been a couple.

With Patsy still in his arms, Chase walked down the porch steps and then made his way over to Anna Mae's car.

"What are you doing here?" he asked. He didn't really care what the reason was. He was just glad that Annie was standing in front of him.

"This afternoon when we were…earlier you said you weren't going anywhere."

"That's right."

"What did you mean by that?"

"Exactly what I said."

"Chase Johnson, are you telling me you're back in Storm to stay? I want to know the truth."

A smile tugged at his lips. "Is that important to you?"

"Yes, it is. You can't just come back into my life after forty years and sweep me off my feet and then leave again. I won't have it."

"I'm not leaving, Annie. I'm looking forward to more days of dancing with you. And if you'll have me, I'm really looking forward to loving you."

Her eyes widened with hope and it nearly broke his heart. He didn't know if it was fair to put her through what was surely to come if they gave their love another go of it. But he did know it wasn't his call to make. He'd come home and in coming home, he'd opened his heart to everything he'd shut out of it years ago.

"Dammit, Chase, don't play with me."

He held the kitten in one hand and scooped Anna Mae up

against his body with his other. "Are you sure you don't want to play?"

She giggled and wrapped her arms around him. Her moist kisses on his cheek and mouth felt cold against the night breeze but made him feel alive. He'd once thought that being on stage, playing his music for people was the only way he could feel alive. But here in Anna Mae's arms, he felt like a young man again and had never felt more alive in his life.

"I love you, Anna Mae Prager."

"I've never stopped loving you, Chase Johnson. We have a lot of time to make up for."

He wagged his eyebrows. "I've got a perfectly good truck sitting right there. We could make up for lost time right now."

She giggled and kissed his mouth and the years melted away. Whatever the future held, he could handle it. He was home.

* * * *

Anticipation flowed through Hector Alvarez as he drove into the parking lot of Henry's convenience store. The owner of the store was the brother of a man Hector had worked with briefly who ended up doing time for aggravated assault on a coworker. The man had a temper that fired with the slightest spark. He was an asshole. But he knew how to get the goods and there was no way that Hector was going back into Storm without reinforcement.

He walked into the convenience store and looked around. A young girl stood behind the counter ringing up someone else's purchases. She wore a low-cut white shirt that showed off her dark-colored bra and all the assets God had given her. If one of his daughters ever dared to show herself in public like that, Hector would have chained her in her room. Men were pigs when it came to slutty women. There was no need to show off your goods unless you wanted to get fucked.

"Is Buddy here?" Hector asked the girl.

She didn't look up at Hector, which annoyed the shit out of him. She continued to ring up the customer's purchases.

Hector took a step toward the counter and pushed his way in

front of the customer, who glared up at him with anger.

"Is he here?" Hector said louder.

The girl snapped her gum and sighed. "In the back of the store by the shed. He's staying out there."

"Thanks," he said.

The bitch rang up the last item and then looked at him with disinterest. "He hates to be bothered."

"I'll keep that in mind."

Hector walked out of the convenience store, went around the building until he saw an old shed with a dusty sedan parked next to it. There was a small window high on the door of the shed, enough for him to peek inside and see that someone was there.

Instead of opening the door, Hector fisted his hand and knocked two times hard, then took a wide step back.

The door opened quickly. If he'd been standing closer, it would have knocked him over with the force of the man behind it.

The scowl on the man's face quickly turned to a smile. "Hector. Long time."

"Buddy. Have you got what I asked for?"

"Do you have the money?"

Hector pulled a stash out of his shirt pocket and showed the man.

"Come inside and I'll show you something pretty," Buddy said.

It took a second to adjust to the difference in light. The shed was small but it was lit with a bright yellow bulb in the middle of the rafters. At the far end of the shed, Buddy had a table set up with guns of every size and caliber spread out.

Buddy smiled as Hector studied the table. "I get a hard-on every time I look at these."

Hector picked up a revolver. "Is it marked?"

"They're all clean."

After a quick check of the gun, Hector said, "This will do." He handed Buddy the money and headed for the door.

"Nice doing business with you, Hector."

Hector turned back. "Get yourself a woman, Buddy."

He walked to his car, listening to Buddy's harsh laugh at his back. He smiled as he climbed into the car. As long as Dakota kept his secret, his arrival in Storm would be a surprise. He couldn't wait to see the look on Joanne's face when she realized he was home.

* * * *

The story continues with Episode 4, Lightning Strikes by Lexi Blake.

About Lisa Mondello

New York Times and *USA Today* Bestselling Author, Lisa Mondello, has held many jobs in her life but being a published author is the last job she'll ever have. She's not retiring! She blames the creation of the personal computer for her leap into writing novels. Otherwise, she'd still be penning stories with paper and pen. Her book The Knight and Maggie's Baby is a New York Times Bestseller. Her popular series includes Texas Hearts, Dakota Hearts, Fate with a Helping Hand and the new Summer House series. Writing as LA Mondello, her romantic suspense, Material Witness, book 1 of her Heroes of Providence series made the *USA Today* Bestseller List and was named one of Kirkus Reviews Best Books of 2012. You can find more information about Lisa Mondello at lisamondello.blogspot.com and sign up for her newsletter to receive new release information at http://eepurl.com/xhxO5.

Sign up for the Rising Storm/1001 Dark Nights Newsletter
and be entered to win an exclusive lightning bolt necklace
specially designed for Rising Storm by
Janet Cadsawan of Cadsawan.com.

Go to www.RisingStormBooks.com to subscribe.

As a bonus, all subscribers will receive a free
Rising Storm story
Storm Season: Ginny & Jacob – the Prequel
by Dee Davis

Rising Storm

Storm, Texas.

Where passion runs hot, desire runs deep, and secrets have the power to destroy...

Nestled among rolling hills and painted with vibrant wildflowers, the bucolic town of Storm, Texas, seems like nothing short of perfection.

But there are secrets beneath the facade. Dark secrets. Powerful secrets. The kind that can destroy lives and tear families apart. The kind that can cut through a town like a tempest, leaving jealousy and destruction in its wake, along with shattered hopes and broken dreams. All it takes is one little thing to shatter that polish.

Rising Storm is a series conceived by Julie Kenner and Dee Davis to read like an on-going drama. Set in a small Texas town, *Rising Storm* is full of scandal, deceit, romance, passion, and secrets. Lots of secrets.

Look for other Rising Storm Season 2 titles, now available! (And if you missed Season 1 and the midseason episodes, you can find those titles here!)

Rising Storm, Season Two

Against the Wind by Rebecca Zanetti
As Tate Johnson works to find a balance between his ambitions for political office and the fallout of his brother's betrayal, Zeke is confronted with his brother Chase's return home. And while Bryce and Tara Daniels try to hold onto their marriage,

Kristin continues to entice Travis into breaking his vows...

Storm Warning by Larissa Ione
As Joanne Alvarez settles into life without Hector, her children still struggle with the fallout. Marcus confronts the differences between him and Brittany, while Dakota tries to find a new equilibrium. Meanwhile, the Johnson's grapple with war between two sets of brothers, and Ian Briggs rides into town...

Brave the Storm by Lisa Mondello
As Senator Rush's poll numbers free fall, Marylee tries to drive a wedge between Brittany and Marcus. Across town, Anna Mae and Chase dance toward reconciliation. Ginny longs for Logan, while he fights against Sebastian's maneuvering. And Hector, newly freed from prison, heads back to Storm...

Lightning Strikes by Lexi Blake
As Ian Briggs begins to fall for Marisol, Joanne and Dillon also grow closer. Joanne's new confidence spreads to Dakota but Hector's return upends everything. A public confrontation between Marcus and Hector endangers his relationship with Brittany, and Dakota reverts to form. Meanwhile, the Senator threatens Ginny and the baby...

Fire and Rain by R.K. Lilley
As Celeste Salt continues to unravel in the wake of Jacob's death, Travis grows closer with Kristin. Lacey realizes the error of her ways but is afraid it's too late for reconciliation with her friends. Marcus and Brittany struggle with the continued fallout of Hector's return, while Chase and Anna Mae face some hard truths about their past...

Quiet Storm by Julie Kenner
As Mallory Alvarez and Luis Moreno grow closer, Lacey longs for forgiveness. Brittany and Marcus have a true meeting of hearts. Meanwhile, Jeffry grapples with his father's failures and finds solace in unexpected arms. When things take a dangerous turn, Jeffry's

mother and sister, as well as his friends, unite behind him as the Senator threatens his son…

Blinding Rain by Elisabeth Naughton

As Tate Johnson struggles to deal with his brother's relationship with Hannah, hope asserts itself in an unexpected way. With the return of Delia Burke, Logan's old flame, Brittany and Marcus see an opportunity to help their friend. But when the evening takes an unexpected turn, Brittany finds herself doing the last thing she expected—coming face to face with Ginny…

Blue Skies by Dee Davis

As Celeste Salt struggles to pull herself and her family together, Dillon is called to the scene of a domestic dispute where Dakota is forced to face the truth about her father. While the Johnson's celebrate a big announcement, Ginny is rushed to the hospital where her baby's father is finally revealed…

Rising Storm, Midseason

After the Storm by Lexi Blake

In the wake of Dakota's revelations, the whole town is reeling. Ginny Moreno has lost everything. Logan Murphy is devastated by her lies. Brittany Rush sees her family in a horrifying new light. And nothing will ever be the same…

Distant Thunder by Larissa Ione

As Sebastian and Marylee plot to cover up Sebastian's sexual escapade, Ginny and Dakota continue to reel from the fallout of Dakota's announcement. But it is the Rush family that's left to pick up the pieces as Payton, Brittany and Jeffry each cope with Sebastian's betrayal in their own way…

Rising Storm, Season One

Tempest Rising by Julie Kenner
Ginny Moreno didn't mean to do it, but when she came home to Storm, she brought the tempest with her. And now everyone will be caught in its fury…

White Lightning by Lexi Blake
As the citizens of Storm, Texas, sway in the wake of the death of one of their own, Daddy's girl Dakota Alvarez also reels from an unexpected family crisis … and finds consolation in a most unexpected place.

Crosswinds by Elisabeth Naughton
Lacey Salt's world shattered with the death of her brother, and now the usually sweet-tempered girl is determined to take back some control—even if that means sabotaging her best friend, Mallory, and Mallory's new boyfriend, Luis.

Dance in the Wind by Jennifer Probst
During his time in Afghanistan, Logan Murphy has endured the unthinkable, but reentering civilian life in Storm is harder than he imagined. But when he is reacquainted with Ginny Moreno, a woman who has survived terrors of her own, he feels the first stirrings of hope.

Calm Before the Storm by Larissa Ione
Marcus Alvarez fled Storm when his father's drinking drove him over the edge. With his mother and sisters in crisis, Marcus is forced to return to the town he thought he'd left behind. But it is his attraction to a very grown up Brittany Rush that just might be enough to guarantee that he stays.

Take the Storm by Rebecca Zanetti
Marisol Moreno has spent her youth taking care of her younger siblings. Now, with her sister, Ginny, in crisis, and her brother in the throes of his first real relationship, she doesn't have time for

anything else. Especially not the overtures of the incredibly compelling Patrick Murphy.

Weather the Storm by Lisa Mondello
Bryce Douglas faces a crisis of faith when his idyllic view of his family is challenged with his son's diagnosis of autism. Instead of accepting his wife and her tight-knit family's comfort, he pushes them away, fears from his past threatening to undo the happiness he's found in his present.

Thunder Rolls by Dee Davis
In the season finale ...

As Hannah Grossman grapples with the very real possibility that she is dating one Johnson brother while secretly in love with another, the entire town prepares for Founders Day. The building tempest threatens not just Hannah's relationship with Tucker and Tate, but everyone in Storm as dire revelations threaten to tear the town apart.

Lightning Strikes
Rising Storm, Season 2, Episode 4
By Lexi Blake
Now Available

Secrets, Sex and Scandals …

Welcome to Storm, Texas, where passion runs hot, desire runs deep, and secrets have the power to destroy… Get ready. The storm is coming.

As Ian Briggs begins to fall for Marisol, Joanne and Dillon also grow closer. Joanne's new confidence spreads to Dakota but Hector's return upends everything. A public confrontation between Marcus and Hector endangers his relationship with Brittany, and Dakota reverts to form. Meanwhile, the Senator threatens Ginny and the baby…

* * * *

Hector Alvarez sat in his car watching the house he'd bought, the one he'd provided for his family. He'd been the king of that castle until the damn sheriff had decided to come in and take what belonged to Hector.

He could still feel the humiliation burning in him, still see that bastard standing over him and telling him to get out of town or he would tell the town what he'd seen.

What had Dillon Murphy seen? He'd seen Hector dealing with his wife. Joanne was his. His. He had the right to deal with her any way he saw fit. He was the one who had put up with her for years, dealt with her lazy ways. Joanne required a firm hand.

The door to the house opened and he saw a man walk out.

Marcus. Marcus had come home. His only son had walked out, leaving his family for some ranch in Montana. Hector had thought it was a stupid fit at the time, a rebellion, but then Marcus had stayed away.

Now he was back and his son looked like a man. Marcus held the door open and smiled down at the girl who walked through.

Mallory. His youngest. Such a pretty girl, but far too influenced by her mother. She wouldn't amount to anything because Joanne had ruined her. It seemed like it was his wife's goal in life to make their children as weak as she was.

Mallory strode off, a bag over her shoulder. She walked down the street with a smile on her face. Like nothing was wrong with the world. Like she was happy.

Like she didn't miss her father at all.

Marcus moved to his car, opening the door for his other sister.

Dakota. His baby girl. Now there was a daughter. He stared at her. Of all the things he'd done, leaving Dakota actually made him feel a little guilty. She was the only one who took after him, the only of his children to truly see him as he was. Dakota understood.

She slipped in the car and then Marcus took off.

It was not lost on Hector that the sheriff's squad car was sitting in front of his house.

Was Dillon Murphy inside trying to take his place? Trying to get his wife in bed?

Rage threatened to take over, the emotion rolling in his gut.

1001 Dark Nights

Welcome to 1001 Dark Nights… a collection of novellas that are breathtakingly sexy and magically romantic. Some are paranormal, some are erotic. Each and every one is compelling and page turning.

Inspired by the exotic tales of The Arabian Nights, 1001 Dark Nights features *New York Times* and *USA Today* bestselling authors.

In the original, Scheherazade desperately attempts to entertain her husband, the King of Persia, with nightly stories so that he will postpone her execution.

In our version, month after month, each of our fabulous authors puts a unique spin on the premise and creates a tale that a new Scheherazade tells long into the dark, dark night.

For more information about 1001 Dark Nights, visit www.1001DarkNights.com.

On behalf of Rising Storm,

Liz Berry, M.J. Rose, Julie Kenner & Dee Davis would like to thank

~

Steve Berry
Doug Scofield
Melissa Rheinlander
Kim Guidroz
Jillian Stein
InkSlinger PR
Asha Hossain
Chris Graham
Pamela Jamison
Fedora Chen
Jessica Johns
Dylan Stockton
Richard Blake
The Dinner Party Show
and Simon Lipskar